The sky was a deep, somber black, and the full array of stars shone down, as if the aurora had never existed.

Michael stared up at the sky. The flare couldn't be over. Solar storms didn't just *stop* like that. *Hypothesis,* some part of his brain thought. *If the aurora has disappeared, then . . .*

His eyes flicked toward the compass on the dashboard. The needle, which had been ramrod straight for their entire trip, now wandered around aimlessly.

"What was that?" Lilith asked. "What's going on?"

"The magnetic field," he said hoarsely. "It's—it's gone."

Also by Christopher Swiedler

The Orpheus Plot

IN THE RED

CHRISTOPHER SWIEDLER

HARPER
An Imprint of HarperCollins*Publishers*

In the Red

 For information address HarperCollins Children's Books, a division of HarperCollins Publishers, 195 Broadway, New York, NY 10007.
www.harpercollinschildrens.com

ISBN 978-0-06-289442-7

Typography by Michelle Taormina
22 23 24 25 PC/BRR 10 9 8 7 6 5 4 3
❖
First paperback edition, 2021

for my father

1

BY FRIDAY AFTERNOON, after a week of careful thought, Michael Prasad had come up with just one theory for how he might make it to Monday morning without getting grounded for the rest of his life.

Hypothesis, he thought. *Parents might be so excited to find out you've succeeded at something that they forget they said you absolutely positively under no circumstances were allowed to try.*

That was a stretch, he had to admit. And it raised the obvious question of whether he would have been better off sitting in the library studying for his Martian history exam, like he'd told his mom he was doing, instead of standing near the main colony airlocks with his helmet under his arm. Based on the puzzled looks he was getting, he wasn't the only one wondering why he was here. Michael was too old to be with the crowd of grade school kids clutching their parents' hands, and he was too young to be one of the high schoolers talking and laughing down by the airlock doors. Michael kept his face expressionless. Why would he care what anyone else thought? He wasn't here to make new friends.

Michael walked over to the end of the plaza, where the transparent dome that covered Heimdall marked the edge of the colony. The sky outside was bright pink from end to end. On a nearby landing pad, a big cargo jumpship sat slightly askew as workers in environment suits repaired one of its landing legs. Little mounds of red sand piled up like anthills against the base of the dome, shifting back and forth in the wind.

He reached out and pressed his fingers against the smooth, icy-cold surface of the dome. The transplastic bent slightly at his touch, and when he pulled his hands back, ten small indentations remained. Slowly the material stretched back into its original shape, leaving no sign that it had ever been disturbed.

"You can touch it?" asked a red-haired boy, who looked like he was around nine or ten years old. He was standing a few meters away, watching Michael with an amazed expression, as if he'd just seen some kind of magic trick.

"Sure," Michael said. "It won't hurt you."

The boy reached out and ran one finger over the surface of the dome. He pulled it back quickly and rubbed his hand against his pants. "It's cold!"

"Well, it's minus sixty outside," Michael said.

"I've only been outside twice," the boy admitted. "But I've done a lot of simulations."

"You'll be fine," Michael said, because he knew this was the sort of thing he was supposed to say to a kid who was nervous about taking the suit test. The boy nodded, clearly reassured. But all of this felt backward to Michael, as if he were in some kind of alternate universe. Someone was supposed to be here reassuring *him*, not the other way around.

"How old were you when you went outside for the first time?" the boy asked.

"Six."

The boy's eyes went wide. Even in Heimdall, most six-year-old kids were playing soccer or swimming in the colony pool, not going out onto the surface. Of course, most kids didn't have Manish Prasad for a father. Michael was pretty sure if they'd made environment suits for toddlers, his dad would have taken him outside before he could walk. He'd gone with his dad on dozens of hikes and camping trips, from Mount Olympus to Valles Marineris and everywhere in between. At this point, all of those trips out on the surface were a jumbled blur—except for the very last one, two years ago. *That* one was still crystal clear.

The boy nodded at the high school kids. "Are you with them?"

"No," Michael said, his face flushing. "They're taking the advanced suit test."

Thankfully, the boy didn't follow up with any questions about why Michael actually *was* here. "My mom says the basic test is easy," the boy said. "She's a jumpship pilot, so she knows what she's talking about."

Michael wanted to tell the boy that his mom was right: the basic suit test was easy. Environment suits were safe, especially the fully automated ones they gave kids. All they wanted to do was make sure that you wouldn't panic once they removed your tethering line. Every kid on Mars took the test when they were ten years old, and nobody failed it.

Almost nobody failed it.

One of the older kids did a handstand and then flipped back down to his feet. The other high schoolers laughed and cheered. If any of them were anxious, they certainly weren't showing it. *Hypothesis: for some people, the more nervous they get, the more relaxed they appear.*

He shook his head. *Hypothesis: for some people, the more nervous they get, the more stupid hypotheses they come up with.*

"I have to go," the boy said, looking back at the younger kids, who were gathering around an instructor. "Nice to meet you."

Michael gave him a little salute. "Good luck."

He stood near the crowd of kids and parents and listened as the woman explained how the test would run. Even two years ago, the instructions had seemed laughably basic compared with the things his father had taught him. Michael remembered looking around at the other kids and wondering whether any of them would freak out when they were outside the dome. It hadn't even occurred to him that *he* might be the one to panic.

Michael's handheld screen vibrated in his pocket. He pulled it out and unfolded it. *Incoming call from Peter Prasad.* Relieved that it wasn't his mom or dad, Michael tapped the accept button and his older brother's face appeared. Peter, with his brown eyes and hooked nose, looked so much like their father that it was sometimes unnerving. Michael, on the other hand, had inherited just enough of his dad's dark skin and his mom's thin features that he didn't look like either one of them. At least over a video link he and Peter were eye to eye and his brother couldn't loom over him the way he liked to do in person.

"If you're going to try to change my mind, don't bother," Michael said.

"So you're really going to do it, huh?" Peter said, somehow managing to look both amused and concerned at the same time. "You don't think it's a good idea to tell Mom and Dad first?"

"No," Michael said. "I don't."

That conversation was one that he'd already had a dozen times over the past year. *Someone with your condition* was the precise phrase his mom liked to use. Someone with his condition shouldn't go out onto the surface. Someone with his condition should stay inside the domes where it was safe. And someone with his condition certainly had no business taking the environment suit test again. She always put a little emphasis on that word *again*, just to remind him of what had happened the first time.

"Is Dad home yet?" Michael asked.

"He called and said he'd be late. He was trying to get everything wrapped up at the station."

Michael pursed his lips. "Wrapped up" was a good term for it, except that his dad had it backward: it was the work that had *him* wrapped up. When their dad had taken the job out at the magnetic field station, their mom had given them a big talk about how it was an important position and how they needed to support him. The magnetic field created by the station protected everyone on the planet from solar radiation, so sure, it was important. But Michael also knew that his dad would be just as wrapped up if someone has asked him to clean the Heimdall colony dome with a squeegee. It was just how he was.

"Well, when he comes home, don't tell him where I am. I want to surprise him."

"Surprise him? Michael—"

"Just don't say anything to him, okay?"

Peter sighed. "Look, I know what Dad promised you. But maybe he didn't mean it exactly the way you think."

"He *did*," Michael insisted.

"Fine. But don't be surprised when Mom and Dad lock you in your room for the next three years."

Peter reached toward the camera and the connection went dead. Michael crumpled up the screen and shoved it back into his pocket. His brother didn't understand. How could he? Everything was perfect for him. He was going to go into the Rescue Service academy next year. Everyone said he was born to be out on the surface. He didn't have a *condition*.

"Gotta get through," he heard a familiar voice say from the other side of the plaza. "Pardon . . . sorry about that . . . excuse me."

Down by the entrance, his friend Lilith was pushing her way through the crowd, ignoring the annoyed looks from some of the parents. Lilith had immigrated from Earth a few years earlier, and she still moved with the awkward bouncing steps of someone who wasn't quite used to Mars's lower gravity. Her blond hair was pulled back in a ponytail and fastened with a rubber band.

"Sorry—gymnastics practice ran late," she said as she jogged over to him. She stopped and scrunched up her face. "Are you okay? You look like my hamster at her vet appointment."

"I'm fine."

"Mmm. You need to relax." She rubbed his shoulders as if he were a low-gee judo wrestler. "What's the nineteenth digit of pi?"

"Four," Michael said.

"What's the weight of Saturn?"

"Five hundred sextillion tons. Except that it doesn't really have a weight, since—"

"Whatever," she said. "What's the surface area of the colony dome?"

That one was harder. "Fifty-six and a half square kilometers," he said after a moment. "Assuming it's a perfect half sphere six kilometers across."

"You've got this sewn up," Lilith said. She jerked her head toward the high schoolers. "How many of those kids even know what the cube root of twenty-seven is?"

"Three," Michael said automatically.

"Three? You think?" She squinted dubiously at them.

"No," he said. "I mean the cube root of twenty-seven is three."

Lilith laughed. "See? You're a lock."

She put her hands against the dome and peered out

at the Martian landscape. "Aren't you worried about that big solar flare everyone is talking about? I mean, is it even safe to go out there?"

Michael glared at her. Was she *trying* to make him nervous? He really didn't need to add anything else to his list of things to worry about. He was about to reply when a voice interrupted him.

"Hey," someone called. "You there, with the helmet."

Michael turned and saw a man in an environment suit walking toward him with his helmet in one hand. The man had the leathery skin of someone who had spent too much time in high-radiation environments, and his hair was shaved down to a thin white stubble. Both of his eyes were artificial, and they made a faint whirring sound as they flicked back and forth.

"You're here to take the test, right?"

"Yes," Michael said, surprised.

"Then come on. We're about to get started." The man jerked his head in the direction of the airlock.

Michael looked around and saw that all of the other kids were gone, and the only other people left in the plaza were parents. He must have missed the announcement that the test was starting. His stomach clenched and he swallowed hard.

"Break a leg," Lilith said, pushing him gently in the direction of the prep room. Seeing his confused stare, she frowned. "That doesn't make much sense, does it? It's an Earther thing. It means good luck."

"Thanks," he mumbled.

He picked up his helmet and walked into the room the man had indicated. Suits were hanging from racks and helmets of various sizes were stacked in narrow cubbies behind the benches. Dusty boot prints crisscrossed the floor, and the acrid smell of the Martian atmosphere hung in the air. But instead of a crowd of younger kids, the only people inside were the four teenagers he'd seen earlier. Michael stopped in the doorway and looked around in confusion.

"I hope there aren't any questions about metamaterials," one of the boys said, pulling an environment suit down from a rack. He was wearing a T-shirt for an Earther band that Michael vaguely recognized. "I can't keep any of that straight."

"I spent all weekend trying to memorize the pressure tables," said the other boy. "Seventeen point two, thirty-three—no, forty-three point eight . . ."

"You don't have to memorize that stuff, nummer. They let you look it up."

A tall, broad-shouldered girl looked through the racks with a disgusted expression. "I really, really wish they'd let us wear our own suits."

The other girl turned toward Michael. "Are you looking for someone?" she asked. She had long black hair and a nice smile.

Michael shook his head. "I'm here for the test," he stammered.

"You're in the wrong place," the boy in the T-shirt said. "This is the advanced test. It's not for little kids."

"How old are you?" the dark-haired girl asked.

"Twelve," Michael said. "But—"

"You have to be at least sixteen, don't you?" one of the boys said.

"No," the dark-haired girl said. "I read that a ten-year-old got her advanced certification once."

"Bollocks to that," said the boy in the Earther T-shirt. "I'm not taking this test with a little kid."

"Poor Beecher," the dark-haired girl said. "Worried that a twelve-year old is going to beat you?"

"I'll beat his face in if he doesn't get out of here," Beecher said, glaring at Michael.

Michael backed up a few steps and nearly ran into the white-haired man. "Whoa," the man said. "Is everything okay?"

"This isn't right," Michael said. "I'm supposed to be taking the basic test."

The man raised his eyebrows. Michael could see the

thought going through his head: why was someone his age signed up for a test for ten-year-olds? Shrugging, the man nodded at the doors to the other airlock.

"I think you're too late. The test for the younger kids has already started."

"Too late?" Michael echoed. After all this, he'd missed his chance to get his certification? "Isn't there some way I can take it? I can't wait until the fall. I have to do it *today*."

"They're strict about starting on time, I'm afraid," the man said. "But if you want, you can come out with us, and I'll give you your basic certification."

Michael looked at the high school kids. It didn't really matter how he passed the test, did it? Going out with the advanced group would probably be more interesting than listening to someone teach a bunch of kids the right way to put on a helmet. And what was the alternative? He wasn't going to go home without his certification.

"Okay," he heard himself say.

Michael followed the instructor back inside and sat down on a bench with his helmet in his lap. He could feel the older kids staring at him. The white-haired man closed the prep-room door and cleared his throat.

"Listen up. This is the advanced suit exam administered by the Martian Emergency Rescue Service. My name is Randall Clarke. I've spent most of my life in a suit. I've worked on Luna, in the Belt, and here on Mars.

Five years ago, I lost my lungs, my eyes, and my eardrums in a pressure suit accident off of Vesta. All of which has apparently convinced someone that I'm qualified to determine whether any of you actually know how to handle yourself out on the surface.

"Any questions?"

Nobody spoke.

"Then grab a suit and get ready. Full checks—hoots to boots." Randall rolled out a privacy screen that divided the prep room into two sections. "Boys on this side, girls over there."

Nervously, Michael walked along the rows of suits, looking for one in his size. "Here you go," Beecher called from the other side of the room. Michael turned and was hit in the chest with a wadded-up suit. "Grade school size, just for you."

Michael ignored Beecher's chuckle and held up the suit. It was probably the closest to his size that he was going to find. He took off his clothes and fastened the suit around his legs and body. The wrist screen was a little bigger than he was used to, but the controls were all familiar to him.

"How much air do we need in our tanks?" one of the girls asked from the other side of the screen.

"No tanks," Randall said. "We're going to use filters only, just like you'd do on a long trip out."

That was something Michael hadn't expected to worry about, since the basic test used standard tanks. But his dad had always preferred to use air vests and filters on camping trips, so Michael was familiar with how they worked. He grabbed a vest from a hook on the wall as Randall passed out carbon dioxide filters. Out of habit, Michael checked the saturation level on the filter, and then he slid it inside the port on the back of the suit's collar. Without a tank, he would be relying on the filter to suck in CO_2 from the atmosphere and convert it to breathable air, since the liquid oxygen in the vest was only enough for emergencies.

He picked up the clear bubble-shaped helmet he'd inherited from his brother. Its smooth transplastic surface was a little yellowed with age, but it was still in good shape, and it was familiar to him. This morning he'd gone over its seals and insulation four or five times, but out of habit he checked everything again.

"Suit's a little big, eh?" Randall said from behind him, adjusting the straps on his air vest. "But don't worry about it. Henrik Arnason never had one that fit right. He was so short they had to stand him on boxes for the publicity photos."

Michael nodded. It was a nice thing for Randall to say. But when Henrik Arnason became the first person to walk on Mars, he hadn't had to worry about a *condition*, had he?

Michael stared at the helmet with a sense of dread. *You've done this before,* he told himself.

Yes, a voice in the back of his mind replied. *And how did that go for you?*

He took a deep breath and pulled the collar over his head. As soon as it sealed against his suit, everything went silent, and all he could hear was the tinny echo of his own breathing. Cold sweat dripped down the back of his neck. He hated this moment most of all. He fought the urge to tear the helmet off and suck in deep lungfuls of fresh air. After what seemed like an eternity, the suit powered on and the sounds of the room came back, relayed from microphones in his collar. The air filter hummed, and fresh air flooded into his suit. He opened his eyes and saw Randall watching him.

"Everything all right?" Randall asked.

Michael fidgeted. He didn't want Randall to see how nervous he was. "I'm fine," he said, trying to sound confident. And it was the truth, wasn't it? All he needed to do was keep his nerves under control, and everything would be okay.

Randall tapped the collar of Michael's helmet, where the name PRASAD had been stenciled in black letters. "You're Manish Prasad's kid?"

Michael blinked in surprise. "Do you know my dad?"

Randall chuckled. "I was surprised when he let them

talk him into running that field station. He never seemed like the type for a desk job. I was even *more* surprised when he convinced me to come along."

"You work for him?"

"I help out at the station, which mostly means making sure the scientists don't forget to put on their helmets before they go outside. But everyone in the Rescue Service knows your dad. Has he ever told you about how he fixed that leak in the old Hesperia habitat in the middle of a dust storm?"

Michael shook his head. His dad hardly ever talked about the things he'd done in the Service.

"Well, ask him sometime. Though I bet he's pretty busy these days, isn't he? When I left the station this morning, everyone was pretty worked up over this flare."

The flare? Michael looked at the airlock doors uneasily. He knew it was supposed to be a big one, but his dad hadn't mentioned anything about it the last time he'd called. Was that why he hadn't come home on time?

Randall double-checked everyone's suits, pointing out any safety checks they'd missed or settings they'd gotten wrong. When they were all ready, he led them through a set of doors into the airlock itself. The hair on the back of Michael's neck stood on end. *Stop it,* he told himself. *You're not even outside yet.*

When they'd all gathered inside, Randall closed the

inner doors and pulled down on a large metal handle. Their suits crackled and stretched as the air pressure around them dropped to match the atmosphere outside. The gauge on the wall settled at four thousand pascals, and the status light on the wall blinked green. The outer doors rumbled open. A thin slice of sunlight cut across the floor of the airlock, shining through a swirling cloud of dust.

Michael's heart pounded in his chest. It was one thing to look out at the surface through the dome of the colony, but it was something else to actually *be* outside, surrounded by nothing but poisonous air, wearing a scratched-up helmet that seemed to be growing smaller by the second. Was the air in his suit already getting stale, or was that just his imagination? He took a deep breath and exhaled slowly. He didn't care what stupid disorder his doctor said he had. He didn't care what had happened two years ago. *He wasn't going to let himself panic.*

Slowly the dust settled, revealing a long ramp that led up to the surface. Little drifts of copper-colored sand collected against the sides of the ramp, shifting back and forth in the wind. A sign at the top read You Are Now Leaving the Heimdall Atmospheric Containment Zone.

"Here we go," Randall said, and stepped out onto the Martian surface.

2

ONE BY ONE, the students followed Randall down the ramp and out onto a small footpath that led away from the colony. Michael trailed behind, squinting in the late-afternoon sunlight. The ground around the airlock had been graded and cleared until all that was left was a fine sand that gathered in little mounds against the colony dome. An eight-passenger rover with the Rescue Service logo stenciled on its doors was parked nearby.

Michael stomped his feet and waited for the heating elements in his suit to catch up with the intense cold of the atmosphere. He took a deep breath and looked back at the colony. Lilith was standing just inside the dome, watching him. She mouthed, "Are you okay?" and he responded with a cautious thumbs-up.

Randall gathered all of the students in a semicircle. "When I point to you, say your name."

The girl with the black hair gave a quick wave. "Marika."

"Bee-cher," the boy drawled.

"Kyle."

"Michael."

"Vivien," the broad-shouldered girl said, but her voice came out as a deep, muffled baritone. Her eyes widened and everyone laughed.

"Anyone want to guess why her voice sounds like that?" Randall asked. "This isn't part of the test, by the way."

Michael waited a moment to see if anyone else would answer. "Her comm unit isn't adjusting for the low pressure."

"Right. That's how we'd all sound if our acoustic systems didn't compensate for the Martian atmosphere." Randall took out a small air gun and cleaned a sensor on her suit. "Try now."

"Vivien," she said, and brightened at the sound of her voice.

"So can anyone tell me why we use these acoustic systems, even though they're short-range and constantly get plugged up with dust?"

"Because sometimes radios don't work?" Kyle offered.

"That's true, though if your radios are busted, you're in a crap storm of epic proportions," Randall said. "Any other ideas?"

"Because they give you a sense of the speaker's distance and direction," Michael said.

"Exactly. It's the same reason we wear these fishbowl helmets. When someone is shouting at you to get the hell out of the way, you don't want to be spinning in circles trying to figure out where they're coming from."

They linked up their radios to the frequency Randall specified. His voice became sharper and more direct, as if he were standing just over Michael's shoulder. As Randall began to explain how the test would be run, everyone's suits beeped.

"Those alarms are courtesy of the massive solar burp that started hitting us yesterday," Randall said. "Be thankful—ten years ago, a flare this size would have had everyone huddled under a meter or two of solid rock. Now that Mars has a magnetic field, all we get are mild radiation warnings. And as a bonus, some beautiful northern lights."

Randall went down the line, checking everyone's suits one last time, and then he lined them up next to the dome. "All right. Time for some drills. Michael, you can follow along if you want. It'll be good practice, if nothing else."

Randall first made them apply patches that would seal a tear in the fabric of their suits, and then they paired up and practiced applying inflatable splints for broken legs.

He simulated different problems with their air units, from imbalanced gas levels to low-pressure warnings, and had them fix each problem.

Michael was pleasantly surprised to discover that he was already familiar with most of the drills. Some of them his dad had shown him back before his panic attacks had started, and others he'd learned when he'd helped Peter prepare to take the advanced test last year. And when Randall showed him something new, it didn't take him long to master it.

"You're sure you were here to take the basic test?" Randall asked after Michael had demonstrated how to reconfigure his suit radio to account for interference. "You know this stuff better than some recruits at the academy."

Michael blushed. "I read the field manuals, that's all."

"I bet," Randall said, chuckling.

"So are we going to try changing out a bad air filter?" Kyle asked. He reached back and tapped the hoses on the back of his neck, as if that were something he did regularly.

Randall shook his head. "Too dangerous. Once you take off your vest, you have less than a minute of air left in your suit, and hot-swapping in a new one is harder than it looks. As it happens, the Rescue Service would prefer that I *not* kill any of my students."

A deep rumble ran through the ground, startling them. It took Michael a moment to locate the source: a jumpship on a landing pad had just fired its main engine. Randall, Michael, and the other students shielded their eyes from the glare and watched as it lifted off.

"Cargo hopper," Randall said as the ship retracted its legs and climbed upward on a pillar of blue fire. "Big one."

"Where do you think it's headed?" Vivien asked.

"Port Meridian," Michael said automatically. Randall and the other kids looked at him in surprise. "I mean, it's heading southeast. And with that trajectory, it's not making a short hop. So *probably* Port Meridian."

"Could be," Randall agreed with a smile. "But we're not here for ground control training. Everyone jump in the rover. Kyle, you're first up."

They climbed into the vehicle, with Kyle in the driver's seat and Randall next to him. Michael sat next to Marika, in the third row of seats. The rover's big tires reached up almost to his shoulder. Marika fastened her seat belt and pulled at the roll bar that stretched over their heads, as if testing its strength.

"If I'd known we were going to have to *ride* with Kyle driving, I would have stayed in bed," she whispered, winking at Michael.

At Randall's direction, Kyle backed the rover out of the corral and out onto a concrete roadway. After about a kilometer, they turned off the road and onto the rough Martian terrain. Michael checked his pulse on his wrist screen. It was a little elevated, but not too bad. He flexed his fingers. So far, so good.

"So what gives?" Marika asked. "First you say you're here for the basic test, and then it turns out you know all this stuff better than any of us."

Michael felt the blood rushing to his face. "I didn't mean to—I mean, I just—"

"It doesn't bother me," Marika said, waving her hand. "I'm just curious. You're Peter's brother, right? I didn't recognize you at first."

"You're friends with him?" Michael asked, making a face.

Marika laughed. "Kind of. So why haven't you gotten your basic certification yet?"

"I tried when I was ten." He looked back at the colony dome, which was quickly receding behind them. Why was he telling her this? "I made it about fifty meters from the airlock before I puked and passed out."

"Oh," she said. "My aunt is like that. She can't put on a helmet without having a panic attack."

Michael winced. "Sorry," Marika said. "So why are you out here, then?"

That was a question Michael had never really considered. He supposed that he could just give up and spend his life inside the dome. He tried to think of the simplest explanation.

"Well, my dad is a Rescue Service officer."

Marika nodded. "I can see how that would make things complicated."

"What about you? Why are you taking the advanced test?"

"Honestly, I don't really like being out here at all," she said. "I'd rather be back in the school geology lab. But the internships at the colony research center require an advanced cert so they can send us out to collect samples."

Soon the colony had disappeared entirely and they were completely alone, with nothing but reddish-brown dirt in all directions. The wheels of the rover were able to sense and adapt to any rocks smaller than a soccer ball, and Kyle did a good job steering around all of the larger boulders or gullies that would have given the rover trouble.

Beecher, on the other hand, seemed to have never driven a rover before in his life. When it was his turn to drive, he zigzagged back and forth over the landscape, avoiding obstacles that Michael wasn't sure were actually there and yet still managing to hit larger rocks that made the rover bounce up and down. When Randall finally told him to stop the rover, Marika gave such a comic sigh of relief that Michael had to bite his lip to keep from laughing out loud.

Marika climbed forward into the driver's seat. Beecher elbowed his way past the other kids and slumped down next to Michael without fastening his seat belt. Michael kept his face straight and his eyes ahead.

When Marika and Vivien had both completed the driving test to Randall's satisfaction, he turned back and nodded at Michael. "You want to try?"

It was clear Randall was just being polite, since rover driving certainly wasn't a part of the basic test. Michael was about to tell him no when Beecher spoke up.

"Him? I'll bet he can't even reach the steering wheel."

Michael glared at him and started to climb up front. "I can drive better than you."

He'd driven smaller rovers with his dad, though of course that had been years ago. But the controls were all the same, weren't they? He slid the seat forward so he could reach the pedals, and Beecher chuckled in amusement. Michael ignored him and shifted the rover into drive and went through Randall's exercises without any trouble.

"It's like being driven around by a leprechaun," Beecher called from the back seat. "Maybe he can find us a pot o' gold."

Michael glanced in the rearview mirror and saw Beecher smirking at him. He pushed down on the throttle pedal and sped up to twenty kilometers per hour. He held it there for a few seconds, and then he jammed his foot on the brake.

"Aah!" Beecher shouted. He hit the seat in front of him with a loud thump and crashed down onto the floor.

Randall grabbed the dashboard to brace himself. He frowned at Michael.

"Sorry," Michael mumbled, staring at the steering wheel. "Thought I saw a rainbow."

A flicker of amusement flashed across Randall's face. He turned around in his seat. "Is everyone okay back there?"

Beecher climbed back into his seat and muttered something inaudible.

"That, people, is why you always wear your safety harness," Randall said. "Michael, swap seats with me."

Randall climbed into the driver's seat and turned the rover north. He drove quickly, speeding around a series of small hills and into a long, wide valley.

"Quiz time," he said over the radio. "Vivien. What's the vapor pressure of water at zero degrees? Quickly, now."

"Six hundred pascals?" Vivien said.

"Six eleven," Randall corrected. "Beecher. How do you recognize a static slope?"

Randall led them through a whole series of questions. What's the rule of thumb for knowing whether water will freeze or sublimate? What's the blood toxicity level for carbon monoxide? Carbon dioxide? Methane? What are the symptoms of decompression sickness? When would you switch a suit to hyperbaric mode? If a student didn't know the answer right away, Randall would bark another name. To Michael, this part of the test was the easiest so far—if there was anything he knew well, it was science.

"Come on, guys, you should know this," he said several times. And then, often as not—"Michael, help them out."

They reached a narrow trail and followed it for half a kilometer until it opened up into a circular area about twenty meters across. Environment suit helmets were laid out on the ground in neat rows. They climbed out of the rover and stood at the edge of the clearing.

"Does anyone know where we are?" Randall asked.

"This is one of the colony cemeteries," Marika said. "The helmets are where they've buried people's ashes."

The dusty helmets stared back at Michael like the heads of decapitated corpses. His skin felt clammy and cold. He folded his arms and looked down at the ground.

"That's right," Randall said. "It's a good place to remind you of all the ways Mars can kill you."

He gathered a handful of pebbles and knelt down. "First: air poisoning." He dropped one of the rocks on the ground. "A tear in your suit, a busted air unit, or a saturated filter. If it's fast, CO_2 poisoning will kill you in minutes. If it's slow, it'll be headaches, vomiting, and hallucinations. And *then* it will kill you."

Michael shifted his feet uneasily. The air in his suit suddenly seemed stale. He checked the gauges on his wrist display and forced himself to take a deep breath. Everything was fine. The test was almost over. He just had to make it back to the colony and everything would be fine.

"Hypothermia." Randall dropped another pebble. "It's minus sixty Celsius right now, and without proper heating systems, you'll freeze to death in minutes."

Michael grimaced. Why was Randall going through all of this, *here* of all places? Did they really need to be reminded of how dangerous Mars was?

Randall added another rock. "Radiation. We've got the magnetic field shielding the planet now, and there's a lining in your suit that'll give you some protection, too. But even just a few years ago, getting caught out in the open in a flare like this would mean radiation poisoning in a bad way. Major organ shutdown, loss of consciousness, and death."

He tossed down the final rock. "Last one: old age. If you're lucky, you'll die out here under the sun and sky. These suits are the best coffins ever made."

A chill went through Michael's spine. His eyes were drawn irresistibly to the rows of helmets. Without even meaning to, he counted them: eight rows of twenty-two helmets. One hundred seventy-six people. How many of them had died peacefully in their beds? How many had died out here on the surface, from hypothermia or air poisoning or any of the rest?

Michael realized that while he'd been staring at the helmets, Randall had been giving them their next set of instructions. Something about navigation satellites?

"Sorry, can you repeat that last part?" Michael asked.

Randall grunted. "I said that once you get your waypoints, you have thirty minutes to find the markers and make it back to the airlock. Make sure you bring all three flags with you."

It was the navigation part of the test. Michael tried to reconstruct what he'd missed. Apparently they were supposed to work out a route without their nav computers? That meant they would have to plot their position using stars and navigate with dead reckoning. Michael wondered how the kids would manage all of that. He'd practiced celestial navigation with his dad, but the best plot he'd ever done was almost a kilometer wide—and that had been from a park on the north side of the colony, underneath the dome.

Randall pulled Michael aside. "This is the last bit. You can ride back with me in the rover if you want."

"You mean I passed?" Michael said eagerly.

Randall snorted. "The basic certification? You passed that half an hour ago. I would have sent you back in, but I wanted to see how you did with the advanced test."

So Randall hadn't just been including him out of politeness—he'd actually been judging Michael along with the older kids. Michael tried to wrap his head around this new bit of information.

"Your other option is to finish the navigation course. If you do that, then I can give you your advanced certification," Randall said.

The words "advanced certification" echoed in Michael's ears. His parents would have been surprised enough if he came home having passed the basic test. How would they react when he told them he'd gotten his advanced certification years early? Even Peter hadn't done that.

"Sure," Michael said. "I can do it."

"All right, then," Randall said. "Good luck."

Randall transferred a series of coordinates to everyone's wrist screens. The courses all led back to the airlock where they'd started. Michael's route would be marked by blue flags.

It had been years since Michael had tried to take a star sight. But he'd read and reread the official Rescue Service guide on celestial navigation, and he knew the theory backward and forward. Confidently, he began to plot his current position. First he sat down on a rock and turned on his helmet filter to block out the light from the sun. The sky darkened and a half dozen stars appeared. Using his helmet's heads-up display, he marked the positions of Sirius, Vega, and Canopus. By taking those measurements and applying a fair bit of math, he could calculate a set of circular areas on the map on his wrist screen. If he did everything correctly, his position would be someplace inside the area where the circular plots overlapped.

But he'd barely begun the process for the first star when Marika jumped up and ran off to the west. Michael stared after her. How had she finished so quickly? He thought he was pretty good at math, but still, it took time to work out an accurate plot. Was there some trick to it that he'd never learned?

A few minutes later, Kyle ran off, followed by Vivien. Michael double-checked his calculations. He needed to be certain that he had this right, or he'd be wandering around the surface for hours.

"See you later," Beecher said, and sprinted away.

"Michael?" Randall asked.

"Almost done," Michael said. He finished his plot and compared it with the waypoints Randall had given him. His stomach churned. The area he'd calculated as his current position was so large that it was almost useless. According to his plot, the first waypoint might be four meters away, or it might be four hundred. How was he going to use this to follow the route Randall had given him?

He only had twenty minutes left. There wasn't time to try to get a more accurate position. He worked out the best course he could and jogged off to the southwest.

After a few hundred meters, the ground dipped into a low basin that seemed to swallow up everything. The clouds had disappeared and the dusty yellow sky was flat and featureless. The only sounds were the crunch of his boots in the sand and the faint hiss of his air filter.

When he'd gone half a kilometer, he stopped and looked back. He should have found the marker by now. Clearly, he'd gone in the wrong direction. How did Randall to expect them to find such exact locations using only star fixes? It was like telling someone to find a particular tree by telling them which forest it was in.

He took another star sight and recalculated his position. From his best guess, the first flag was a half kilometer north of where he was. He set off again, running as fast as he could.

He tried to stay calm, but in the back of his mind he could feel a tiny kernel of panic beginning to grow. He shouldn't have tried to finish the advanced test—he should have just ridden back to the colony with Randall. Michael pushed the thought away and concentrated on his breathing. In and out, in and out. Steady. Smooth.

He was only a short distance from the colony, and he was perfectly safe. He wasn't going to fail this test because of a stupid panic attack. He wasn't going to fail just because his brain couldn't tell the difference between real danger and fake danger.

When he figured he'd gone another half kilometer, he stopped and recalculated. It was probably to the east, now. Or it could be south, or north, or west. It was hopeless. He kicked a boulder so hard his toe hurt, and then he stood there, his breath hissing through his nostrils.

Are you finished? he asked himself. *Or are you just going to stand here kicking rocks?*

He clenched his jaw. There *had* to be a way to find his position without using his computer. He climbed up onto the boulder and looked around. No flags in sight, blue or otherwise—just a picturesque view of the buildings and towers of Heimdall, a few kilometers away.

Michael sucked in his breath. That was the answer! He activated the zoom on his helmet. The colony seemed to leap toward him, and he scanned back and forth until he found the airlock. His helmet rangefinder read 3,708 meters. He checked the compass: 211 degrees, south-southwest.

With those measurements, all he needed was a little trigonometry to work out his position. The distance to the airlock gave him the hypotenuse of a right triangle, and its direction on the compass gave him one of the angles. He typed quickly on his wrist screen, and in a few moments he knew his current position down to the meter. Which meant the first waypoint must be . . .

He turned to the east. Sixty meters that way.

He sprinted forward, staring intently at the ground ahead of him. Something caught his eye: a little blue flag. He'd found the first waypoint.

Michael stuffed the flag in his belt. Now that he knew his location, finding the other waypoints would be easy. The only question was how long it would take him to get the rest of the flags and make it back to the colony. He checked his screen. Only five minutes left.

He ran north, taking long, fast strides. He picked up the second flag and rechecked his position. Only one waypoint left. The air in his suit was thick and heavy, and his eyes had a hard time focusing on the map on his screen. Cold sweat dripped down the back of his neck.

Not now! He couldn't have a panic attack now. Three hundred meters northwest for the third waypoint. He vaulted over rocks and gullies, his boots barely touching the ground. He reached down and grabbed the third flag at a dead run and turned toward the colony.

His lungs pumped in and out, trying to pull as much oxygen from the air as they could. Flecks of saliva spattered over the inside of his helmet. In the distance he could see people gathered outside the airlock, but his mind was so flooded with panic that he'd forgotten about Randall and the test and the other kids entirely. Everything faded away until all that was left was an overwhelming desire to get inside where it was safe, where he could *breathe.* Nothing else mattered.

His foot caught on a rock and he crashed to the ground. He tried to push himself to his feet, but his legs refused to cooperate. A gigantic hand was squeezing his chest, and his breath came in short, heaving gasps.

"Michael?" Randall asked over the radio. "Are you okay?"

No, Michael tried to say, *I'm not okay,* but his stomach lurched and vomit sprayed over the inside of his helmet. A dull roar echoed in his ears like the sound of a million voices laughing at him. The sound grew louder and louder until it swept over him like a flood, and then everything went black.

3

MICHAEL SAT ON the edge of the hospital bed with his arms folded across his lap and stared at the white tile floor. His throat was raw and his mouth still tasted like puke, but he hardly noticed.

He'd failed. He'd completely and utterly failed. Instead of proving that he was better, that he could actually take care of himself out on the surface, he'd done exactly the opposite. He had shown everyone that they were right—that the only place he belonged was inside the colony.

Michael could feel his mom watching him from the chair in the corner of the exam room. Her gray-blue eyes were tired and her cheeks were pale. She was still wearing a peach-colored blouse with a security badge from her job in the colony's health department, a few floors above in the building they were in now. The only time she'd spoken since she'd arrived was when she'd asked Michael if he was okay. Since it was clear from her tone that in this case "okay" meant "not on the verge of death," he'd just nodded, and that had ended the conversation.

"So this has happened before," the doctor said, scanning through Michael's medical history on a handheld screen.

"Yes," Michael said in a monotone.

"Anxiety is like a safety mechanism in your brain," the doctor said. "In the right amounts, it's beneficial. If people weren't anxious about heights, we'd have to treat a lot more broken necks."

She paused, clearly waiting for him to smile at her joke, but Michael just stared at the floor and kept his face expressionless.

"Sometimes, those safety mechanisms malfunction. They provoke your body into a panic response even when there's not a real threat. The problem in your case is that when you're out on the surface, the panic *itself* is a threat. Colloquially, this is called suit anxiety, though really it's a kind of panic disorder."

Michael pursed his lips. He hated the term "disorder" even more than "condition." It made him sound so weak and helpless.

The doctor flipped to a new page on her screen. "I see he's been going through cognitive behavioral therapy with Dr. Chapman."

"Yes," his mom said.

"Well, physically, there's nothing wrong with him," she said, putting a slight emphasis on *physically* that made Michael clench his teeth. "There's no reason to keep him here any longer. However, I strongly recommend that he stay inside the colony from now on. He was lucky today that there were people around to get him back through the airlock. The next time, things could be a lot worse."

"I understand," Michael's mom said, in a tone that implied she would be doing a lot more than just keeping him inside. "Thank you."

She stood up and shook the doctor's hand. Michael followed her out into the hallway and down toward the hospital toward the hospital's main doors. The atrium was empty, and the clacking of her shoes on the polished granite floor echoed all around them. Outside, the sky was dark and the air was chilly. The buildings around the hospital plaza, lit from below by spotlights, seemed to peer down at them. They crossed the plaza and climbed into one of the tram cars lined up on the curb. Michael settled into his seat and steeled himself for the volley of anger that he was sure his mother was about to hurl at him.

But after she told the car the address for their house, his mother just leaned her head against the window and stared out at the passing streets. He watched her nervously. Not only was she not shouting at him, she wasn't saying anything at all. Was she just biding her time, or was she so upset that she couldn't even speak?

The tram car rolled quickly down the city streets toward the northern residential section. Soon they were gliding past cylindrical single-family houses and small commercial shops. Thin trees, the largest no more than a few meters tall, ran along the sidewalk. A few kids playing in the street moved aside so the tram car could pass.

The car rolled to a stop in front of their house and the doors slid open. The flowers that surrounded their front porch shone yellow and pink in the light from the streetlamps. Michael followed his mom up the steps and into the house. She hung her shoulder bag on a hook in the hallway and then went silently into the kitchen. Peter looked up from the couch in the common room with an expression that said, *I wouldn't want to be you* and then turned back to the soccer match on the wall screen.

Michael's dad was standing by the kitchen table holding a mug of tea in both hands. Steam from the tea drifted up around his head and disappeared in the antique glass light fixture that hung overhead. His yellow jumpsuit was dusty and wrinkled. Michael's mom pulled a chair out from the table and looked at him expectantly. He sat down and folded his arms across his lap.

"I just want to know one thing," his mom said to him. "Did you even *think* about how dangerous that was?"

"It wasn't that big of a deal," Michael muttered.

"Do you know what bodies look like when they come back inside? Frozen solid and shriveled up?"

Of course he knew—the last time they'd had this argument, she'd shown him *pictures*. "I don't hear you telling Peter to stay inside."

"Hey," his brother called from the living room. "Leave me out of this, okay?"

"Peter is older. Peter has had more training." She didn't even bother to add the most important point: Peter didn't have a *condition*.

"She's right, Michael," his dad said. "You could have gotten yourself seriously hurt."

"But I didn't," Michael insisted.

"That's not the point!" his mom said. "We talked about this, over and over. We agreed that you weren't ready."

"*You* agreed."

His mom's face tightened, but she didn't take the bait. Instead she got a glass out from the cabinet and jammed it underneath the water dispenser until it was full.

"Randall said he'd give me my basic certification," Michael said to his father. "I would have passed the advanced test, even, if I hadn't spent so much time taking star sights."

"Star sights?" his dad said, surprised. "Why didn't you just use your nav computer?"

"Because it wasn't allowed," Michael said. Suddenly his mouth went dry. Randall *had* said that, hadn't he?

"Of course it was. How could anyone navigate a course like that without a nav system?"

Michael sagged back in his seat. Now it made sense why everyone had found their flags before him: they'd all used their wrist screens. He'd completely misunderstood the test. It would have taken him just a few minutes to get all the flags if he'd known he could use his computer. He would have been back at the colony before anyone else. He wouldn't have had a panic attack. He would have passed the advanced test *easily.*

"If you didn't use your computer, then how did you find the flags at all?" his dad asked.

Michael explained how he'd measured the angle and distance to the airlock to find his starting point and get to the first flag. He shrugged. "After that it was just dead reckoning."

His dad was silent for several seconds. Finally he nodded. "That's certainly a . . . *unique* approach."

Unique? Michael looked at his father in confusion. Was unique good or bad?

"The test isn't the point," his mom said. "I don't care if the Rescue Service pins a stupid *medal* on your chest. Until your doctor says you're okay, you're staying inside the colony."

"That's not what Dad told me," Michael blurted out angrily. As soon as he said it, he clenched his mouth shut. *Stupid*, he told himself. *Stupid, stupid, stupid*.

"What?" his mom said, surprised.

His dad cocked his head to one side. "Michael, what are you talking about?"

"You promised me at the beginning of the school year that if I got my certification, I could come visit you at the station this summer." The words jumbled together, but he pressed on, knowing that he had to get it all out now. "I did it, Dad. I almost passed the *advanced* test, even. . . ."

He trailed off, trying to read his dad's expression. He remembered, didn't he? He had to remember.

They'd been walking home from school after the science fair when his dad had started talking about how someday soon everything would go back to normal. He'd said that when Michael got his certification, he could come out to the station for a whole week over the summer holidays. He'd gone on and on about how they could go for hikes around the glacier and watch the auroras at night.

"I did say that," his dad said, and then paused. Michael's heart thumped so loudly that he was sure they could all hear it. "But what I meant was that we'll do all of that someday. When your doctor says you're ready."

Michael felt dizzy, as if the entire world had suddenly been turned upside down. Someday? When was *someday*? His doctor had already said that he might never completely stop having panic attacks. What if she never thought he was ready?

"But you told me," Michael said, in a voice that was almost a whisper. "You *told* me."

"I know," his dad said. "But you have to understand . . ."

He didn't go on, but he didn't need to, because now Michael did understand. His dad had told him all of those things to make him feel like his suit anxiety was something temporary, like pneumonia or a broken leg. But it wasn't—it was a part of him. He wasn't ever going to be able to go out on the surface like a normal person, and his dad knew it. All the things that he'd said before were just lies.

Because what kind of a promise was it if you knew that you would never have to keep it?

"Dr. Chapman says she's very impressed with how far you've come," his mom said, in a suddenly gentler tone. "We just have to keep at it."

Michael looked away. Through the window he could see the lights of the colony center glittering against the night sky. He was twelve years old. He wasn't going to cry.

"Is there anything else?" he asked woodenly.

His mom looked at his dad, and then she sighed. "No. You're excused."

Michael walked slowly up the stairs to his room. Above his door was the small green placard telling rescue workers that someone inside couldn't use a normal suit and might need special care in an emergency. The window in his room was open, and the model spaceship over his desk swayed gently in the breeze from the colony air circulators. The wall screen flashed to life as he entered the room, showing a panoramic view from one of the research stations on Titan. He smacked its power button, and it went dark.

As he sat down on his bed, his screen vibrated with an incoming call. He glanced at it and swiped his thumb across the accept button. "Hey, Lil," he mumbled.

"Hey," Lilith said, looking at him with a concerned expression. "So are you okay?"

"No," he said simply. He didn't know whether she meant okay in the physical sense or just okay overall, but it didn't really matter, because pretty much nothing was okay.

"I guess your parents didn't take it too well?"

"You could say that, yeah."

"I'm sorry."

"Whatever," he said. "It's no big deal. I'll talk to you later."

He stuck his screen back under his pillow and lay down. The night air was cold and he wrapped the blankets around his shoulders. Everything he'd been working toward for the past year was ruined. All of his plans for the summer, all of his plans for the rest of his *life*. Everything.

What was he going to do now?

Early the next morning, he woke up to the sound of his parents arguing downstairs. He lay motionless, staring at the faint gleam of sunlight on the wall, and tried to make out what they were saying.

". . . my job . . . ," his dad said, and then something that ended with ". . . the station."

"I understand, Manish," she said. "But *he's* the one you're going to have to explain it to."

His parents moved toward the back of the house, and their voices grew indistinct. Michael curled himself up in a ball. He hated it more than anything when his parents fought like this. Sometimes he thought it might be better if they'd just have their arguments right in front of him, so that at least he'd know what they were fighting *about*.

He waited until he heard the sounds of breakfast in the kitchen, and then he got out of bed. When he got downstairs, Peter was eating a bowl of oatmeal at the table. Michael looked around. "Where's Dad?"

Peter jerked his head toward the front door. "He just left."

"He *left*?" Michael echoed. "But he just got here!"

"He said he had to get back to the station," Peter said, shrugging.

Michael slumped down into one of the kitchen chairs. It was Saturday morning. His father had been home for less than twelve hours. What could possibly be so important that he had to go back *now*?

Peter went over to the auto-pantry and came back with a second bowl of oatmeal. He set it down on the table, but Michael just stared at it silently. He didn't have any appetite at all.

"So you really got all the way through the advanced test?" Peter asked. "Without any studying or anything?"

"*Almost* all the way," Michael mumbled.

"I'm pretty impressed, to be honest," Peter said through a mouthful of oatmeal. "That's a tough exam. I never would have thought my nummer little brother could do it. It must have taken a lot of guts. Especially for someone with your . . . whatchamacallit. Disorder."

"I thought maybe Dad would be impressed."

Peter shrugged. "Maybe he was. He can be hard to read sometimes."

Hard to read? Everything about their dad seemed pretty clear to Michael. Make easy, empty promises.

Come home for just long enough to break them. Then leave the next morning to do the things that were *actually* important.

"Well, whatever you do, don't give up, okay?" Peter said. "Don't let anyone convince you that you're some kind of freak."

"I *am* a freak," Michael mumbled.

"No," Peter said firmly. "You're not. I don't care how many panic attacks you have."

"Mom and Dad don't see it that way."

"Mom and Dad just want to protect you, because that's their job," Peter said. "But part of growing up is deciding when you don't need protection anymore."

This was a side of Peter that Michael hadn't seen before. He was used to his brother telling him what to do, or what not to do, usually with a punch in the arm for emphasis. He was still trying to figure out how to respond when their mom came down the stairs carrying a box of cables and electronics junk. "Morning, boys."

"Dad already left," Michael said.

She set the box down on the table. "I know. He didn't want to. He was up all night talking to people back at the station."

Michael scowled and folded his arms. Why was his mom acting like it was perfectly okay for his dad to fly right back to work on a Saturday morning?

"I've got to head to the track for conditioning," Peter said, standing up and heading for the front door. He talked all the time about how he was going make the first-string soccer team when he started his senior year in the fall. "If you make pancakes, save some for me, okay?"

The door closed, leaving the house silent and still. Michael's mom sat down next to him. "Pancakes—you know, that's not a bad idea. I think I still have some of the real maple syrup Uncle Robert sent from Earth."

"I'm not hungry."

They sat quietly for a moment. Michael kept his eyes on the table. His mom was trying to smooth everything over, but he wasn't going to fall for it. He was nothing but a walking, breathing *condition*. How were pancakes going to fix that?

"I'm not happy that you took the test without talking to us," she said. "But I think I understand why you did it."

Michael snorted. "You *think* you understand?"

"You don't have anything to prove, Michael. To me, or your dad, or anyone else. There's nothing wrong with you."

Michael pushed back his chair and stood up. "If that's what you think, then you don't understand at all." He stomped up the stairs and paused in front of his room, staring at the green warning placard. Scowling, he pried it off the wall and hurled it down the stairs into the kitchen, where it landed against the wall with a satisfying *clang*, and then he slammed his door.

In the afternoon, when the house was quiet, Michael came back downstairs and headed out the front door. He didn't know exactly where he was going, but he knew that he didn't want to be at home anymore. He sat on a swing at the school playground for a little while, watching some younger kids run around playing tag on the soccer field, and then he peered in through the window at his sixth-grade classroom. The school term had just finished a few days before and the room hadn't been cleaned out yet. Posters for their class unit on biology still hung on the walls, and a small holographic image of a beating human heart rotated slowly above its stand on the teacher's desk.

How could his dad have lied to him like that? He'd told Michael exactly what he wanted to hear, even though he knew it wasn't the truth. It would have been better if his dad had just not said anything at all, instead of making Michael think that everything was going to go back to normal.

Eventually Michael found himself walking down the street where Lilith lived. Her house wasn't hard to spot, even from a few blocks away. Instead of the standard red or brown Mars tones of the rest of the neighborhood, her house was yellow with pink trim around the windows, a style that she insisted was popular in Miami. Most new colonists made at least some effort to fit in, but Lilith and her mom seemed determined to bring everything about Earth along with them. Once they'd cooked actual real-meat steaks, sent here at some crazy cost by Lilith's aunt. The smell had made Michael want to vomit, but Lilith and her mom had eaten them like they were a delicacy. Last month they'd insisted on installing a *birdhouse* in their backyard, even after he'd patiently explained that the nearest bird was in the Port Meridian zoo, over ten thousand kilometers away. But somehow Lilith and her mom did all of this with an enthusiastic, contagious zeal that was impossible not to like.

When he arrived, Lilith was sitting on the front porch. She had the sort of carefully neutral expression that he'd seen before when she'd been upset about something. She looked up and gave him a thin smile as he approached.

"Hey," she said. "Good to see you out and about."

"Sorry for hanging up on you yesterday." He sat down cross-legged in the grass. "Everything okay?"

"Sure. Why wouldn't it be?" Her smile broadened, but he could tell that it was forced.

Her front door opened, and Lilith's mom appeared. She was tall and pretty, with long hair that she dyed a different color every week and was currently a bright shade of blue. Her jaw was set and her mouth was in a tight line. "Beccy says that—"

She stopped when she saw Michael. Immediately her angry expression disappeared and was replaced by a warm smile. "Oh—hello, Michael. I didn't realize you were here."

"Hi, Ms. Colson."

"Want some tea?"

Pouring tea over ice and adding a ridiculous amount of sugar was the one Earther custom that Michael had discovered he quite liked. But he could tell from Lilith's expression that she wasn't in the mood, so he just shook his head. "No, thanks."

"All right. Let me know if you need anything."

She let the door slide closed, and Lilith sighed. "Sorry. She's a little manic today."

"Is everything okay?"

"Oh, yeah," she said, waving her hand. "Just normal Colson family stuff. What about you? How are you feeling?"

"I'm fine," he said. "But are you sure that—"

"It was scary seeing you like that," she went on. "They took you away on a stretcher. I got into a wrestling match with one of the medics, but they still wouldn't let me come with you."

"It wasn't a big deal," he said, shrugging. "Just a little panic attack."

"If that was a little panic attack, then I don't ever want to see a big one," Lilith said. "So why don't you ever talk about it? I mean, I know you didn't pass your basic certification that first time you tried. Was that because of a panic attack, too?"

"Yeah," he said. "That was the first time it happened."

It had been a lot worse, too, because he'd had no idea what was happening. All of a sudden it had seemed like his body was going haywire. He couldn't breathe, couldn't think. . . .

"Before that, you were fine?"

"I went outside with my dad all the time when I was a kid. I had over a hundred hours on the surface by the time I was ten. Then I go to take the test, and . . ." He pantomimed an explosion with his hands. "I tried a few more times with my dad, but I never even made it out of the airlock."

"That's so *weird,*" she said, squinting thoughtfully. "I wonder what started it."

Michael shrugged. That was what he'd asked his

doctor, over and over, but all she would say was that *anxiety can surface at any time* and *there isn't always an explanation.*

"Well, we'll figure it out," Lilith said firmly. She stood up and stretched. "But right now, I have to go get ready for tonight."

"What's tonight?"

Her eyes twinkled. "Wait and see."

4

THAT NIGHT MICHAEL dreamed that he was on Phobos. The little moon moved quickly across the face of Mars, brushing past the enormous peak of Olympus and skimming along the narrow scar of Valles Marineris. Beyond the planet there were no stars, only the blackness of space. He was cold and tired.

His suit chimed with an incoming call. He tried to find the controls to answer, but his vision was turning gray. The chime sounded again, more insistently this time, and then he was slipping down, down, down. . . .

He hit the floor of his room, still wrapped up in blankets and clutching his pillow. His screen was flashing on his bedside table. *Incoming call from Lilith Colson.* He squinted at the time. 0045.

"Accept call," he mumbled. "Lilith? What's going on?"

"I'm outside," she said. "Open your window."

Michael stood up with his blankets still wrapped around him and slid the window open. The cool night air made him shiver. He leaned his head out and saw Lilith standing in the grass below him.

"What are you doing here?" he asked in a raspy voice.

"I told you," she said. "We have plans. Meet me out front."

"But . . . it's the middle of the night."

"You're very perceptive," Lilith agreed. "As my aunt used to say—nighttime is the ally of the mischief-maker."

"You're serious?"

"Yes, I'm serious," she said patiently.

"Where are we going?"

"You'll see. Meet me out front, and be quiet about it. Remember—silence is the ally of the mischief-maker."

She ran around toward the front of the house. Michael blinked away sleep and stretched his arms. He was certainly awake now. There was no way he was going back to bed anytime soon, at least not without finding out what Lilith had been planning.

He got dressed in a T-shirt and sweatpants and put on his sneakers. He poked his head out into the hallway and listened. The house was silent. As quietly as he could, he padded down the stairs and slipped out through the front door. If his mom caught him sneaking out in the middle of the night, on top of everything else that had happened, he'd never leave the *house* again, much less the dome. He listened one more time to make sure nobody was stirring, and then he closed the door behind him.

Lilith was standing on the sidewalk. The streetlamps cast wide pools of yellow light whose edges almost touched, leaving little corners of darkness.

"Okay," he said. "So what's going on?"

"You'll see. Patience is the ally of the mischief-maker."

With a sigh, he followed her down the street. Everything was quiet except for the faint rustling of trees. She turned onto a small footpath that led to a larger road. A transport truck passed them, momentarily blinding them with its headlights. They turned again, heading down another road that led past a row of fishery ponds. The black water rippled and swirled as salmon crested the surface.

After about a half kilometer, they reached a small industrial zone made up of storage units, processing centers, and other buildings Michael couldn't recognize. Lilith consulted her screen and then led him down a series of alleyways and concrete paths. Finally they stopped at a large garage with two flexible doors that had been rolled up into the ceiling. Lilith pulled out a flashlight and shone it around.

On the far side of the garage, a flatbed truck was suspended on a mechanical lift with various important-looking parts of its engine strewn all around. At the back, a large ramp led down to an underground cargo airlock. The walls were covered with racks of tools, pieces of machinery, and "safety first" posters.

Using her flashlight, Lilith guided him past the bits of machinery and equipment that lay on the floor until she reached a door in the corner of the room. "Close your eyes."

It was clearly useless to argue, so he shut them and let her lead him through the door. "Okay—you can open them."

His first thought was that he was standing directly on the Martian surface. Stretching out all around him was nothing but jagged rocks and copper-colored sand, dimly lit by the vast array of stars above his head. For a brief, terrifying moment he stood rooted to the ground, unable to breathe.

"Michael?"

Lilith's voice brought him back to reality. He looked down at his feet and saw that he was standing in a patch of grass. A few meters ahead of him, the colony dome shimmered where it met the ground, forming an invisible line where the grass was replaced by the rocky terrain of the surface.

"I'm sorry," Lilith said. "This was dumb of me. We should go back—"

"It's fine," he said, keeping his eyes on the grass at his feet. He took deep breaths and waited for his pounding heartbeat to return to normal. They'd come all the way out here in the middle of the night, and he wasn't going to let his stupid panic disorder ruin everything. "I'm okay. Really."

Carefully, he looked around, letting his eyes adjust to the dim light. The buildings behind them didn't quite meet up with the dome, leaving a narrow grassy area like a tiny park. The whole area felt like an afterthought, as if someone had made a mistake when planning out the rest of the colony. A few discarded drink bottles lay in the grass, and graffiti on the wall announced that G.B. Loves H.R. A blue duffel bag was half hidden behind a row of bushes near the door, apparently forgotten or left behind.

"One of the high schoolers on my gymnastics team told me about this spot," Lilith said. "It's beautiful, isn't it? It's like you can see every star ever made. But I didn't realize it would . . ."

"You didn't realize it would make my stupid malfunctioning brain panic," he said. "It's not your fault."

How could anyone expect her to know? Even Michael

didn't know what would trigger his condition. During the test, he'd been outside for over an hour, and everything had been perfectly fine up until the very end. Tonight, he'd almost had a panic attack just from seeing the night sky. How was he supposed to keep his anxiety under control if he didn't know what caused it?

"Your brain isn't malfunctioning. It's just trying to keep you safe."

"It's doing a great job," he said. "One more panic attack and my parents won't ever let me out of my room."

He touched the dome with his fingers. She was right about one thing—it was a beautiful spot. As close as you could come to being out on the surface without actually going outside.

"Wait," he said, turning back toward her. Something had just clicked in his mind. He pointed at the bag behind the bushes. "Isn't that your gym bag?"

"Oh—yeah," she said. There was an odd, nervous tone in her voice. "I guess I must have left it here?"

She went to pick it up, but he grabbed it before she could reach it. He unzipped it and found two environment suits, complete with helmets.

So *that* was her big plan. Not just to come out here to see the stars, but to actually go out onto the surface. Except that now she was so worried about his anxiety that she was pretending like it wasn't what she'd been thinking all along. This was what he hated the most about his condition. One minute, someone was telling him that having panic attacks was no big deal. The next, they were treating him like a porcelain doll that could shatter at any moment.

"I can go outside, you know," he said. "It's not a big deal. And what about you? You don't even have your suit certification."

"Well, actually I do," she said, looking a little embarrassed. "I took the test last month. I wanted to surprise you."

Michael almost laughed out loud. Ever since she'd moved here from Earth, Lilith had been the only other person in his class who didn't have her basic certification. Now even she had gone out and gotten it like it was nothing at all. Because, of course, it *was* nothing at all. People took the test every day without having panic attacks. They went outside every day without needing to be hauled back in on a stretcher.

That wasn't going to be him anymore, he decided, with a conviction that was almost scary. From now on, he wasn't going to let his stupid *condition* stop him. He'd practically passed the advanced test, hadn't he? He knew how to take care of himself. Maybe he'd get panic attacks and maybe he wouldn't, but either way, it would be better than staying inside like a frightened little kid.

"Let's go," he said.

"Are you sure?"

"I'm sure," he said. "First, though—"

He stopped. From the other side of one of the buildings came a harsh bark of laughter, followed by a chorus of giggles and hushes. Lilith grabbed him and pulled him toward the door. Just as she opened it up, however, a group of older kids appeared from around the corner. Lilith jerked open the door, but the beam of a flashlight caught them before they could go through.

"Hey," someone said. "Who's that?"

Michael clenched his teeth. He recognized that voice. It was the older boy Beecher who'd made fun of him. He held his hand up to shade his eyes from the light.

"Isn't that the kid from the suit test?" asked a second voice. Kyle, Michael remembered.

"Seriously?" said Beecher. "The little nummer who puked in his suit?"

"Yes," Michael called out, not knowing what else to say. "It's me."

Beecher and Kyle walked up to them, accompanied by a girl Michael didn't recognize. Beecher grinned at them like a cat who'd caught a couple of mice. Michael had known bullies like him before. Were they just having fun, or were they actually interested in hurting someone?

"What are you guys doing here?" Lilith asked casually.

"That's funny," Beecher said. "I was going to ask what a couple of grade school kids are doing in *our* spot."

"We're in middle school, actually," Lilith said.

"You feeling better, little dinkus?" Beecher asked, peering at Michael with mock concern. "Or are you going to piss in your pants again?"

Taking his cue from Lilith, Michael just shrugged and did his best to look disinterested. "I'm fine."

"You're *fine,*" Kyle repeated. "Well, we're glad to hear that."

Another group of older kids came around the corner, talking in hushed voices. Michael squinted as four more flashlights were aimed in his direction. He was relieved to see them. *Hypothesis: the larger the group of older kids, the less likely that someone will be hurt.* But when the new group was close enough for him to see their faces, his relief faded away. *Hypothesis: the larger the group of older kids, the more likely it is that one of them will be your brother.*

"Michael?" Peter asked, astonished. "What the hell are you doing out here?"

"You know this kid?" Beecher asked.

"He's my brother," Peter replied.

"Hi, Peter," Michael said. "Um . . . good to see you?"

Beecher laughed. "How come you never told us your brother was a blubbering little coward who—"

He didn't get a chance to finish the sentence. Peter

grabbed him by his shirt and shoved him up against the wall of the garage so hard, Michael could hear the dull thunk of his head against the concrete. Now it was Michael's turn to be astonished—he'd never seen Peter so angry. Beecher outweighed him by fifteen kilos, but Peter held him there against the wall as if he were a six-year-old.

"Don't talk about my brother like that," Peter said. "Ever. Got it?"

"Hey," Beecher said, struggling against Peter's grip. "Easy. I was just playing around."

"Good. Then go play over there. I'm going to talk to my brother."

Peter let go of Beecher and turned back toward Michael. Beecher glared at him and muttered something under his breath, and then he punched Kyle in the arm. "Come on."

"Bye, Peter's little brother," one of the girls said with a giggle, as they all headed over to the other side of the little grassy area. "And Peter's little brother's friend," another added.

"See you," Lilith said cheerfully.

"Now tell me," Peter said, in a toneless voice that made Michael nervous. "What exactly are you doing out here in the middle of the night?"

"Just looking at the stars," Lilith said.

Peter looked intently at Michael, who flinched despite his best effort. "Just looking at the stars," Michael echoed.

"Mmm-hmm," Peter said. "You know, Lilith, you're a much better liar than Michael."

Lilith held up her hands in a what-can-I-do expression. "The pope is a better liar than Michael."

"Fine," Michael said. Why did they need to lie, anyway? "We're going outside the dome—"

"Oh, boy," Peter said, pursing his lips. "I was afraid you'd say that."

"—and you're not going to stop us," Michael said.

"I'm not?" Peter asked skeptically.

"He's not?" Lilith said.

"You're not," Michael said. "Because part of growing up is deciding when you don't need protection anymore. Isn't that what you told me?"

"I meant that about Mom and Dad. Not *me*." Peter took a deep breath. "I guess it's kind of hard for me to take the moral high ground here, since I was around your age when I snuck outside for the first time."

"Really?" Michael asked, suddenly very interested in this bit of information. "Where—"

"Of course, there's a big difference," Peter said. "I never had any suit anxiety."

Michael bit his lip. Had he been wrong about his brother? Was even Peter on his parents' side now?

"On the other hand, you know more about being out on the surface than any twelve-year-old I've ever met," Peter went on. "And you're the only one who knows what your panic attacks are really like. So I'm just going to ask you—are you sure you can handle it?"

Michael wasn't sure what his answer would have been if Peter had asked him that just a little while ago. But he'd made his decision. He wasn't going to let his anxiety stop him, no matter what happened.

"I can handle it."

Peter and Lilith looked at each other for a moment. "I trust him," she said, shrugging.

Peter sighed. "I do too—as much as I wish I didn't. Promise me you'll stay safe, and that you won't do anything stupid?"

"Promise," Lilith said.

"This is almost a Prasad tradition now," Peter said, ruffling Michael's hair. "Going outside in the middle of the night with your first girlfriend."

"Oh," Michael said, embarrassed. "She's not my girlfriend."

Lilith stiffened, and there was an awkward silence. Peter raised an eyebrow. "I see. Well, carry on then. And *stay safe*."

He turned and jogged back toward the other high schoolers. Lilith pulled one of the suits out of the bag and tossed it on the ground in front of Michael, and then she shoved a helmet into his arms with so much force that he stumbled backward a step.

"All right, let's get dressed," Lilith said. "I'll go inside. You can change out here."

She closed the door behind her, leaving Michael standing by himself. Why was she suddenly acting so weird? Had he said something wrong?

He went behind the bushes and quickly changed into the suit, ignoring the amused looks from some of Peter's high school friends. As he waited for Lilith, he inspected the helmet she'd brought. It wasn't his, of course, but it was the right size and was in good shape. It would be fine. *He* would be fine.

"I wish they'd make these things a little less skintight," Lilith said as she opened the door again. She shimmied her hips and pulled at the fabric of her suit.

"You're not mad about what I said, are you?" Michael asked. He was getting the distinct impression that "mad" was an understatement for how Lilith was feeling right now. "I mean, you aren't my girlfriend, right?"

"Michael," she said, sighing, "you wouldn't know a girlfriend if one punched you in the face. Now come on."

His head was spinning as he followed her back into the garage. What did she mean by *that*? By the time they'd found two oil-stained air vests and finished hooking up their suits, he'd already considered four different explanations. As they walked down the ramp toward the big cargo airlock, he settled on a fifth. *Hypothesis: sometimes girls say things just to confuse you.*

"Are you doing okay?" Lilith asked.

It took him a moment to realize what she was asking. He'd been so distracted by her comment about girlfriends that he'd hardly noticed the fact that he was now wearing an environment suit and helmet.

"Yeah," he said, trying not to think about it too much. "I'm fine."

They stopped outside the inner airlock doors. Lilith consulted a scrap of paper with some numbers written on it, and then she tapped a code into the panel next to the doors. Michael looked at her quizzically. "My team captain's dad's girlfriend runs this garage," she explained.

They stepped inside and Michael started the depressurization cycle. The air rushed out of the airlock and the pressure display spun downward. The whoosh of the pumps grew fainter and fainter until everything was silent. A red light flashed three times, and the big outer doors slid open.

They walked carefully out onto the surface, their boots crunching through traces of ice in the sand. Everything was dark except for two big circles of light from flood lamps on either side of the door. Stacks of cargo containers cast long shadows like outstretched fingers. A large corral held a half dozen rovers in various states of disrepair.

"Have you ever been outside at night?" Michael asked.

"Nope. First time. Kind of spooky."

They snapped headlamps onto the tops of their helmets and turned them on. The beams were like solid spears of light in the darkness. Michael walked around the outside of the corral, peering at the rovers. Each one had a small printout taped to the side listing the repairs that needed to be made. He stopped near a two-person buggy with a bent roll bar.

"Here we go," he said. "This'll do."

"You want to steal a rover?" Lilith asked. "An hour ago I could hardly drag you out of bed, and now you're pushing grand theft auto. I've created a monster."

"I want to *borrow* a rover," he corrected. "There's something I want to show you. So unless you want to spend two hours walking—"

Lilith held up her hands. "Oh, I'm good."

As he hopped over the fence and climbed into the buggy, he could feel his confidence building. This was exactly what he needed—for people to *listen* to him and treat him like he was any other kid, instead of telling him how he was different.

He sat down and clipped on his nylon safety harness. Lilith paused for a moment to inspect the bent roll bar.

"It's fine," Michael said, glancing briefly at the damage. "Someone was just driving too fast."

He wiped a thin layer of dust off the central control screen and flipped the main power switch. The headlights flashed on and the screen came to life.

"Giddyup!" Lilith cried.

Michael looked at her with a baffled expression.

"It's something my aunt used to say," Lilith said with a shrug. "It means 'Let's go.' I think."

A rush of adrenaline flowed through him as he disengaged the brake and pressed down on the throttle. The tires spun in the dirt, and they lurched out of the corral and onto a small concrete path. When they reached an intersection with a larger road, he stopped and consulted the map display on the rover's console.

"So where are we going?" Lilith asked.

"Shh," he said. "Patience is the ally of the mischief-maker."

She rolled her eyes so dramatically he could practically feel it in his seat. "Uh-huh."

He followed the larger road for a few kilometers and then turned off onto a small rutted trail. They bounced along, kicking up a cloud of dust that glowed pink in the light from their headlamps.

"I seriously think I'm going to die of boredom," Lilith said, yawning.

After a few minutes he slowed down, peering into the darkness ahead. Suddenly Lilith sat up straight and pointed off to one side. "Ohmygod. What was that?"

"Interested now?" Michael asked, grinning.

"Just tell me it wasn't a giant alien cockroach, because I swear that's what I saw."

He turned the rover until the headlights reflected on something metallic. As he drove carefully forward, a large insectlike object emerged from the darkness ahead of them.

"Wow," Lilith said. "What is it?"

Michael stopped the rover. "It's a probe from Earth. It was called Phoenix."

They climbed out and walked carefully the rest of the way, as if a loud sound might wake it up. The main body was just a flat disk with an array of instruments, antennae, and cameras, all hand wired like amateur science experiments. Its two solar panels had both broken off into sharp pieces, and its long robotic arm was twisted and bent. Everything was covered in a fine layer of dust and grit.

"My dad took me here once," Michael said. "When I was only seven or eight. That was the first time he let me run around without my tether."

It was hard to believe that in those days, his dad had always pushed him to do more, more, more. Even after his first few panic attacks, his dad had kept trying, telling him that maybe it was just some kind of allergic reaction to his environment suit. Now, though, it was like he was pushing Michael in the opposite direction. Stay inside. Don't take any chances. Don't try to do anything, because you'll probably fail.

Lilith pointed to a small flat circle on the main body, next to a stencil of the American flag. "What's this?"

Michael crouched down. "I don't know," he said. "It looks like an old data disc."

"I think there's some writing on it, but the dust is covering it up."

"Don't touch it," he said. He went back to the rover and pulled out a compressed-air gun. He turned it to the gentlest setting and blew the dust away. Lilith leaned close and read the words aloud.

"'This archive, provided to the NASA *Phoenix* mission by The Planetary Society, contains the names of twenty-first-century Earthlings who wanted to travel to Mars in spirit, if not in body.'"

"I wonder if these people thought that someday there'd be two kids standing here reading this," Michael said.

"Aren't they sending probes to other stars soon?" Lilith asked. "Maybe in a hundred and fifty years, our great-grandkids will be standing next to one of *them* and talking about how primitive it looks."

Suddenly her face turned pink. "Not *our* great-grandkids. Just yours and mine. Separately."

"Of course," Michael said. "I didn't think—"

"Good," she said.

He sighed and wondered whether he was ever going to understand her. Probably not, he decided.

They sat down cross-legged in the dirt and looked up at the sky. Behind them, the colony dome looked like a child's snow globe waiting to be picked up and shaken. A massive array of stars floated overhead, blue and red and orange and yellow, like flecks of glowing paint splattered across the sky.

"It's so weird that the stars don't twinkle," Lilith said. "I still can't get used to that."

"The atmosphere is too thin."

"And no moon. I miss the moon."

"Mars has *two* moons," Michael said. He pointed to the south. "There's Phobos, and there's Deimos."

"Pfft. Those are just overgrown rocks." She sat up and dug around in her suit pocket. "Oh! Speaking of which—happy suit certification day!"

She handed him a small plastic box. Michael opened it carefully. Inside was a small black rock sitting on a three-pronged stand. The surface of the rock was covered with glittering white veins, like an intricate spiderweb.

"So I know that rocks from the Belt are really the most touristy thing ever . . . ," Lilith said.

He picked up the rock. It was surprisingly light. "I've never seen one like this."

"I know, right? It's volcanic. There's a theory that asteroids like this were once a part of Mars."

"I've never heard that."

"Okay, well, it's *my* theory," she said. "Anyway, maybe someday you'll discover an actual Martian volcano and you can start a collection or something."

"There haven't been any active volcanos on Mars for—"

"Michael."

"Sorry," he said. "It's beautiful. Thank you."

For a long time, neither one of them spoke. Michael ran his gloves through the sand, searching for chunks of carbon dioxide ice and then squeezing them in his fingers until they flashed into vapor. Just like him, he thought. Apply a little heat and pressure, and suddenly there's nothing left.

"My dad doesn't think I'm ever going to get better," he blurted out. He didn't mean to say it, any more than he'd meant to *not* say it up until now. It just came out.

Lilith sat up and stared at him. "What are you talking

about? Of course you're going to get better. You already *are* better."

"Well, tell him that." Michael put his shoulders back and deepened his voice. "'My son Peter is just amazing. He's already been accepted into the academy. But Michael? He's got a *condition*. He's never going to be able to put on a helmet without puking.'"

"He didn't actually say that, did he?"

"No," Michael said. "He didn't have to. I could see it on his face. He's ashamed of me. I'll bet he doesn't want me visiting him at the station just because then someone might find out how *useless I am*."

He punctuated the sentence with three hard kicks to an oblong rock that was half buried in the sand in front of them.

"Sometimes a little distance is good," Lilith said. "Me and my dad were a lot happier after my parents separated. Of course, for us, 'a little distance' is a few dozen light-years."

Michael snorted. "Earth is only two hundred million kilometers away."

"Yeah? Seems farther." She tilted her head back and looked up at the stars. "Which one is it?"

"There." Michael pointed up at a pale blue point of

light near the constellation Pisces.

Lilith stood up and cupped her hands around her mouth. "Hey, Dad!" she shouted. "Don't forget my birthday this year, okay?"

Michael's face twitched into a little smile, and Lilith plopped back down. "You don't really talk about your dad much," he said.

She shrugged. "Nothing to talk about, really."

"You and your mom seemed pretty upset yesterday."

"Oh, she was just mad about some stupid stuff he did," she said. "But it didn't bother me."

Lilith might be a better liar than he was, but he could see that there was something she wasn't telling him. "You're sure?"

She paused for a moment, and then she sighed. "All I can say is that parents suck on any planet. Maybe someday, someone will invent something better. Till then we just have to make do."

"I guess. But—"

"I know what'll make things better." She dug around in the pocket of her suit. After a moment she held her empty hand out toward him. Michael looked at her in confusion.

"This is a pretty awesome present. It's what my aunt

gave me when my parents divorced—a one-time-use ticket to do anything you want. Anything at all." She waved her hand at him. "Go on, take it."

Still a little baffled, he pretended to take the ticket from her. "Uh . . . thanks?"

"I used mine to get the best day ever. My aunt and I drove up to the theme parks in Orlando and rode roller coasters until they kicked us out. We ate nothing but ice cream from morning to night. And when we got back, she helped me toilet paper Jenny Bennet-Xi's house."

"I don't think I want to toilet paper anyone's house."

"That's only because you've never met Jenny Bennet-Xi," Lilith said. "But that was *my* perfect day. What would *you* want to do? There must be something."

What would he do, if he could do anything? He knew the answer without even really thinking about it. "I'd drive out to the station at the ice cap, knock on the door, and say, 'Hi, Dad.'"

"That's it?"

"Yeah," Michael said. He kicked the rock in front of him again, causing it to topple over. "Just to show him. Just to see his face. And then I'd turn around and come back here."

Lilith looked thoughtful. She checked her watch and

then sat up straight. "Well, it's already pretty late. We'd better get started."

"Where are we going?" Michael asked, confused.

"Like you said—up to the ice cap. To say hi to your dad and all that."

Michael stared at her. "You mean, right now? Lil, I was kidding!"

"You didn't sound like you were kidding."

"It's two hundred kilometers away! You want to drive for six hours, *tonight?* Just so I can say hi?"

"No," Lilith admitted. "I'd be much happier if you wanted to do something simple, like break into the school and eat ice cream until we pass out. But it's your perfect day, not mine."

"He'll *kill* me. I'll be grounded for years!"

"That's a very good counterargument," she agreed. "But now isn't the time to worry about stuff like that. Now is the time to say, 'This is what I'm doing whether anyone likes it or not.'"

Michael tried to wrap his head around the idea. Go all the way up to the station tonight? Just the two of them? It was crazy. It was *beyond* crazy.

But how amazing would it be to drive all night and show up there at the station as if it were the most normal thing in the world? As if there weren't anything wrong with him at all? Maybe that was the only way to make his dad understand that Michael was more than just a kid with a *condition*.

"You're really up for this?" Michael asked.

"I'll admit—going outside always seemed so boring. But now that we're sneaking away, and if they catch us they'll probably send us to the Belt, it's a lot more exciting, don't you think?" She shrugged. "Also, I think I can go for six hours without peeing."

"*That's* your biggest concern?"

"Well, it's right up there with not-getting-hit-by-a-meteorite."

"All right," he said, taking a deep breath. "Road trip. Isn't that what you call it?"

Her face crinkled. "Road trip."

5

"HOW LONG TILL we get there?" Lilith asked. She had her head resting on the roll bar and her feet propped up on the dashboard.

"Ten minutes less than the last time you asked."

"And you're sure you know where we're going?"

"The autopilot does," Michael said. He pointed at the compass on the dashboard. "And since the station generates the north pole of the magnetic field, the compass points right to it. So it's kind of hard to get lost."

"Humph," she said. "That's too easy. You ought to be following the north star or something."

"Mars doesn't have a north star."

"Seriously?"

"It's tilted at a different angle from Earth, so its north pole points at empty space." He pointed out the constellations of Cygnus and Cepheus and showed her how to find the spot between Deneb and Alderamin that showed true north.

"Neat," she said. "Where did you learn that? From your dad?"

Michael nodded.

"You doing okay? Being out here and all of that?" She said it casually, but he could hear the concern in her voice.

"I'm doing fine."

The strange thing was that it was true. After two years of his parents making him feel as if he would collapse the moment he put on a suit, he'd started to believe it. But here he was, driving a rover in the middle of the night, fifty kilometers from the nearest colony. In a few hours he'd knock on the door to his dad's research station, and everyone would see that they were wrong.

Lilith reached her hand out past the roll bar as if feeling the wind. "Can't this thing go any faster?"

"No," he said. "Not safely, anyway."

She sighed. "Is there anything to eat, at least?"

Michael fished out an energy gel bulb from the compartment underneath her seat. He showed her how to twist the top and shake it until it had warmed up to a drinkable temperature. Cautiously she inserted it through the port in her helmet next to her chin and took a sip.

"Ugh." She held the bulb near the light from the control panel so she could read the label. "That's supposed to be banana pineapple?"

"It's for emergencies. Supposedly you can live on that stuff for weeks."

She took another sip and scrunched up her face. "It tastes like someone put a pile of plastic toys and banana peels in a blender."

Michael was beginning to wonder whether a six-hour trip in a rover together was a good idea. "You can go to sleep if you want."

"Yeah?" she said. "I mean, I wouldn't mind a little nap, but I don't want to leave you all alone."

"I'll probably doze off too," he said. "Go on, get some sleep."

It didn't take her long to take him up on his offer. She curled up in the seat and closed her eyes, and in a few minutes she was snoring.

He double-checked the autopilot and then got out a bulb of drinking water and sucked it dry. The slightly plastic taste brought back memories of one of his first camping trips, when one of their water containers had sprung a leak and frozen solid in the middle of the night. By the end of the trip they'd gone through their rover's entire supply of emergency water and had resorted to chipping off chunks of their frozen water supply and melting them on their little stove so they could wash their hands and faces. It had been a grand trip, even though Michael couldn't remember exactly where they'd gone. Terra Tyrrhena, maybe?

A wisp of bluish-green smoke appeared in the sky directly ahead of them. Michael watched in fascination as it grew larger and larger until it had spread out across the entire horizon like a pulsing cloud. Randall had said that the big solar flare that was going on would cause some beautiful auroras, but Michael hadn't imagined anything like this. Bands of red and blue and green fire rippled and twisted and curled in on themselves until they disappeared. It was the most beautiful thing Michael had ever seen.

He was about to wake up Lilith when his wrist screen beeped. He glanced down and saw a message from his father. *Some amazing auroras up here.*

Michael froze. His mind swirled with conflicting emotions. Eighteen hours ago his dad had suddenly flown back to the station without any explanation, without even saying goodbye, and now he was sending random messages about the aurora? In the middle of the night?

What was his dad even doing up at this hour?

Michael thought for a moment, and then he typed back, *I bet.*

The response from his dad came back quickly. *Thought you'd be out. Did I wake you up?*

No, Michael replied. *Woke up a while ago and couldn't fall back asleep.*

Wish you could see this.

Michael looked up at the aurora, feeling very self-satisfied. He *was* seeing it. He wasn't even inside a station, looking out through a window like his dad probably was. He was out here in the middle of the northern plain, surrounded by nothing but stars and sky.

Maybe soon I can come visit you, Michael wrote back. Soon, as in four hours from now.

For almost a minute his dad didn't respond. Finally a message appeared.

I hope so. And then: *I have to go. Love you.*

Michael sat back in his seat. The breath hissed through his nostrils. That was it? That was all his dad could say—*I hope so*? That was the sort of thing parents told you when they knew something was never going to happen. It was almost as bad as *someday.* He punched the dashboard with his gloved fist.

"Hey," Lilith said, sitting up and looking around blearily. "What was that?"

"Sorry," Michael said. "It was nothing."

"You're sure it wasn't a meteorite?"

"I'm sure. Go back to sleep."

"Okay," she mumbled. "You should sleep too."

She rolled over and closed her eyes again. Michael watched her enviously. He was exhausted, but sleep seemed like it would be impossible. He leaned his head back and watched the aurora and thought about what he would say when he met his dad at the station. "I told you I could do it," maybe. Or "Hey, good seeing you all the way out here." Maybe that was too much, though—maybe he should let his actions speak for themselves. He'd finally decided on a simple "Hi, Dad" when his eyes closed and he drifted off.

He and his dad were standing in an airlock. Early-morning sun streamed in through the windows in the outer doors. Michael was holding his helmet. He put it on and sealed it against his collar. The pumps roared and the outer doors opened. Panic gripped him, cold and familiar. His breaths came in rapid-fire bursts. He saw the silhouette of his father walking out into the sunlight. His gut spasmed, and he threw up.

"Again," his dad said. It was late afternoon. The inside of Michael's suit still smelled like vomit. He put on his helmet and gave his dad a thumbs-up. The doors opened. Michael tried to take a step, but everything was swaying and spinning. He saw the ground a moment before he hit, and then everything was dark.

"Again." It was nighttime. Michael looked at his helmet. A smear of blood coated the inside. He put it on and gave a thumbs-up—

Michael sat up with a jolt. He blinked away beads of sweat and tried to focus his eyes. Where was he? He was wearing a helmet. He was outside.

"Michael," a voice was saying. Someone was shaking him by the arm, trying to get him to wake up. "Michael!"

All at once he remembered: Lilith, the rover, the station, his dad. Michael's lungs gasped for air in an uneven rhythm: *IN out IN out IN out.* The terrified feeling from the nightmare wouldn't go away. He pleaded with himself to calm down. He pulled at the fabric of his suit, trying to relieve the tightness across his chest. What had his doctor told him? *Acknowledge but don't agree,* she had said. *Acknowledge that you are afraid without agreeing that there is any real danger.*

One little part of his brain was terrified. That was

it. One little part was screaming its head off, but there was *no real danger.* A wave of nausea made his stomach clench, and saliva spattered the inside of his helmet as he gasped for air.

"Michael, listen to me!" Lilith said. "What's seventeen times fifty-six?"

He turned his head toward her. Why was she asking this *now?* But even as he stared at her, his mind was working on the answer. "Nine hundred fifty-two," he stammered.

"What's the molecular weight of oxygen?"

"Fifteen," he said. "Fifteen point nine nine nine four."

"How many bones are in the human body?"

"Two hundred six."

"Deep breaths, okay? Just take deep breaths." She squeezed his shoulders and held her helmet against his so that her face was all he could see. He nodded and tried to reassert control, but his breathing still came in rapid-fire gasps.

"Which girl in our class has a crush on you?" she asked suddenly.

"What?" he gasped.

"I said, 'Which girl in our class has a crush on you?'"

It hadn't ever occurred to Michael that *anyone* in their class might have a crush on him. "No idea," he snapped. "How many more stupid questions are you going to ask me?"

"Just one," Lilith said. "How are you feeling?"

He blinked. He'd been so distracted by her questions that he hadn't even noticed that his stomach had relaxed and his breathing had almost gone back to normal. The reddish-black haze of fear that had been threatening to swallow him was back to a tiny wisp in the back of his mind.

"Better," he mumbled. "Thanks."

"Don't mention it," Lilith said, looking eminently pleased that he had.

She handed him a water bulb and he took a long gulp. His skin still felt cold and clammy, but otherwise it was as if the panic attack really had been just a part of his dream.

"Anyway, how do *you* know someone has a crush on me?" he asked.

"For one, because I've got quite the girlish intuition. I notice things."

"Mmm-hmm."

"Also, though, because last week she told Marcy Dagher."

Michael paused. "Really?"

"*Big* crush. Her words."

Michael tried to picture any of the girls in their class saying something like that. "Who was it?"

Lilith shook her head and mimed pulling a zipper across her lips.

"But—"

"Hey, is it normal that the sky is green? Because it's halfway between gorgeously beautiful and totally freaking me out."

He sighed. Lilith could be completely infuriating sometimes. "It's just the radiation from the flare bouncing off the magnetic field. It's perfectly safe."

"Hum," she said, leaning her head back against her seat again. After a few minutes Michael was sure she'd fallen asleep, but suddenly she sat upright again.

"This station is where the magnetic field is generated, right?"

"Kind of," Michael said. "Underneath the station is a giant magnetic inducer. There's some kind of weird quantum reaction with another inducer at the south pole—"

"Weird quantum reaction," she said, waving her hand. "Got it. And the crazy green light definitely isn't dangerous?"

"It's completely harmless. I promise."

She pointed up at the sky. "Then why is it doing . . . that?"

For a moment Michael didn't understand what Lilith was talking about. The aurora was going through one of its phases where it collected into a tangle of bright lines that pulsed and twisted like a massive knot. Then he realized that all of the tendrils of light were being pulled down toward a single spot, as if some unseen force were slowly untangling the knot. Soon all that was left were a dozen flickering lines that converged directly above the glacier.

"That must be where the station is," he said. "We're seeing the magnetic field itself."

He tried to sound confident, as if this was something he'd expected to happen. But inside, he was unnerved. Something about this felt very wrong.

I have to go, his dad had said. What was he doing up in the middle of the night, and why would he have to go so abruptly? Was something happening?

The colorful lines thickened and multiplied, until the sky was filled with dozens of green and red rivers of light that flowed down toward a single spot directly in front of them. The light grew brighter and brighter until only a handful of stars were still visible.

"It's beautiful, I guess," Lilith said, her voice shaking. "But—"

A crackling sound came over the radio, accompanied by a deep hum that reverberated in their skulls. The hum rose in pitch, higher and higher, until they both clapped their hands against the sides of their helmets in a futile attempt to block out the noise.

"What's happening?" Lilith shouted. Her voice was

barely audible over the squeal from their headsets.

Before Michael could respond, the sound intensified, cycling up and down all the way from a high-pitched squeak to a deep rumble like rock grinding on rock. Pain shot through his eardrums.

Then, without any warning, it was gone. The sound, the glow. Everything. The sky was a deep, somber black, and the full array of stars shone down, as if the aurora had never existed.

Michael stared up at the sky. The flare couldn't be over. Solar storms didn't just *stop* like that. *Hypothesis,* some part of his brain thought. *If the aurora has disappeared, then . . .*

His eyes flicked toward the compass on the dashboard. The needle, which had been ramrod straight for their entire trip, now wandered around aimlessly.

"What was that?" Lilith asked. "What's going on?"

"The magnetic field," he said hoarsely. "It's—it's gone."

6

"GONE?" LILITH ASKED. "How can it be *gone?*"

"I don't know," Michael said. His heart raced. If the magnetic field had failed, then as soon as the sun came up, there would be nothing to protect them from the full force of the flare. How much time did they have until the radiation was more than their suits could handle?

"But what—"

"I don't *know*!" Michael snapped.

The nav computer flashed an error. *Primary signal lost.* Then, a moment later: *Secondary signals lost.*

Michael stared at the screen, trying to understand what was happening. If the planetwide navigation systems were already being affected by the flare, then what about communication satellites? Quickly, he switched his suit to the global emergency channel. He heard a brief hum, followed by bits of static and three or four overlapping voices. Then the channel went silent. *Carrier signal lost*, his wrist display said. He tried other channels and got the same result.

"Satellites are going down," he said. "No navigation, no radio uplinks."

"Okay, you're joking, right?" Lilith asked. "This is all some stupid prank? Scare the Earther girl?"

"It's not a prank," Michael said. "We have to find shelter."

"Shelter from what?"

"From the sun!" He pointed at the eastern horizon, where the sky was already starting to brighten.

"You're serious?" she asked.

"Listen to me," he said. "If we're out here when the sun comes up, *we will die*." He could hear Randall's voice in his head. *Radiation poisoning: major organ shutdown, loss of consciousness, death*.

"And we can't call for help?" Panic was creeping into her voice. "How can you and I still hear each other?"

"We're using line-of-sight radios, not satellite uplinks." His eyes widened. *Line-of-sight radios*. Even if they couldn't bounce a signal off of a satellite, maybe they could talk to someone at the station.

He switched his suit to the local-area emergency channel. "Hello? Is anyone there? If you can hear me, please answer."

Ten seconds went by, and then twenty. Lilith watched him intently. He felt sweat trickling down his forehead. "Please. If anyone can hear me—"

"This is Randall Clarke," a ragged voice said. "I can hear you. Who is this?"

Michael's heart leaped. "Randall! This is Michael Prasad. I need help."

There was a brief pause. "Michael? Where are you? And what the hell are you doing out here?"

"I'm with my friend in a rover south of the ice cap. Can you tell me what's happening? The magnetic field—"

"There's been an accident at the station." Randall was breathing heavily, as if he were running. "I can't get many details. I've been out on the east slope."

"An accident?" Michael repeated. "What kind of accident?"

"I don't know. There's a lot of radio interference."

"Is my dad okay?" Michael asked. "Randall, do you know if my dad is okay?"

A woman's voice interrupted. ". . . support teams to the east corridor. All personnel . . ." Her voice broke up in static.

"How far are you from the station?" Randall asked.

"A few hours. Maybe a little less."

"There's not enough time for you to get here," Randall said. "When the sun comes up, the radiation will be lethal. Do you understand?"

"I understand, but—"

"Head straight for the glacier as quickly as you can." Randall's next words were drowned out by static. ". . . or a cave. At least a meter of solid rock . . ."

"Tell my dad where I am!" Michael shouted. "Please, tell my dad!"

The first ray of sunlight peeked out over the horizon. All at once there was a jumble of voices shouting, as if a dozen different channels had been jammed together. "Randall? Can you hear me?" Michael said.

The radio went silent.

"Did you get all that?" Michael asked hoarsely. Lilith gave a barely perceptible nod. Her face was ashen.

Michael shifted the rover into gear and jammed his foot down on the throttle. They sped up a small ridge and then started down a long, rock-covered slope. The rover bounced over each rock and ditch. Michael clutched the steering wheel, and Lilith grabbed onto the roll bar to steady herself. He stole a quick glance at the sun, which was now a bright orange curve on the horizon. How was it rising so *quickly*?

In front of them, the cliffs of the ice cap glowed red in the sunlight. Boulders and debris from ancient eruptions littered the landscape. Lava flows cut wide channels across the ground. Each time they reached one of the deeper gullies or sinkholes, Michael was forced to turn to the left or right until he found a safe spot to cross.

"Keep an eye out for any caves," Michael said. He braked suddenly and swerved around a large rock, and then he accelerated again. "Or overhangs. Anything we can use for shelter."

"Michael . . . ," Lilith said uneasily.

He ignored her and kept his eyes focused on the terrain ahead. Their suits beeped radiation warnings. Michael glanced at the sun, which had almost cleared the horizon. He went through a series of mental calculations. The flare was supposed to peak at around three watts per square millimeter. Their suits could handle about a tenth of that. Given the current angle of the sun, how long would it be before their bodies absorbed a lethal dose? His brain whirred.

"Look out!" Lilith shouted.

A large sinkhole appeared just in front of them, half hidden in the shadow of a massive boulder. Michael turned the wheel sharply to the left and jammed on the brakes. The wheels lost traction and the rover spun around. A second later, the ground disappeared beneath them. For a long moment they were suspended in the air, tilting slowly to one side, in complete silence except for the whistling of the wind. Michael clutched the wheel reflexively and steeled himself for the impact.

They hit the ground with a sickening crunch that threw

them hard against their harnesses. The rover flipped over onto its right side and skidded down the incline, kicking up a cloud of dust that blinded them completely. They hit a rock and tumbled end over end until they finally came to rest. The rover's metal frame creaked and shuddered, and then everything was still.

Michael hung against his harness, the straps digging into his torso, and tried to process what had happened. Was it over? Were they still alive?

Lilith unclasped her safety harness and ran her hands along the surface of his suit, searching for punctures. "Are you okay? Can you walk?"

He nodded. She helped him unfasten his harness and slide down onto the passenger seat. They staggered out between the roll bars. She squeezed his arms and legs and pressed her hands against his ribs to check for broken bones.

"I'm fine," he gasped. The fog in his mind was starting to recede. He quickly checked her suit for tears. "What about you?"

"I'm okay," she said. "But the rover . . ."

Michael limped around the rover and inspected the damage. Its right front section had been crushed inward, and the front axle had snapped in half. Three of the tires were limp and deflated. The frame was bent and mangled.

He sagged down against a rock. What were they going to do now? There was no way they could fix the rover themselves. How could he have been so careless? He'd just wrecked the only chance they had of getting to safety.

A distant part of his brain finished the calculations he'd been working on. *Thirty minutes.* After only thirty minutes of exposure, their bodies would have absorbed enough radiation to kill them.

Lilith grabbed his arm, jolting him out of his thoughts. She pointed at the glacier. "Come on! We need to find a cave, right?"

Michael nodded, still half dazed. He climbed into the wreckage and pulled out all the pouches of water and energy gel that he could find. They stuffed them in the pockets of their suits and scrambled up the steep slope. The faint warmth from the sun on Michael's face made his skin itch. It was just his imagination, he told himself. There wouldn't be anything to feel until later, when the radiation poisoning kicked in and his body started to devour itself.

After a hundred meters, the ground started to slope upward. The black, frozen surface of the cliff was sharp and jagged. Every outcrop and handhold dug into their gloves and boots. If they lost their grip even for a moment they could easily break a bone or puncture their suits.

Lilith pointed up and to their right. "There!"

Michael looked where she was pointing. Something sparkled in the sunlight: a layer of ice running down the slope like a frozen waterfall. They'd reached the edge of the glacier. As they climbed higher, they could see a dark gap in the ice where a wide cave led deeper into the mountain. Lilith scrambled inside and then helped Michael climb up. They crawled toward the back of the cave, skirting around pillars of ice that hung down from the ceiling. Once they were well out of the sunlight, they collapsed against an ice-covered wall, breathing heavily.

"Are we safe in here?" Lilith asked.

He stared at her in confusion for a moment, and then he checked his radiation monitor. "Yeah. We're okay."

Lilith walked around the perimeter of the cave, shining her headlamp all around. The beam reflected eerily from the hanging pillars of ice. She stood at the mouth of the cave and looked out. "How long do you think it will it take for them to find us here?"

"Not long," Michael said. "We're going to be okay. I promise."

She snorted. "For all that brainpower, Michael, you really are a terrible liar."

7

FOR A LONG time they sat without talking. Lilith played a game on her wrist display, occasionally muttering to herself. Michael watched the shadow of the cave entrance creep along the ground as the sun rose.

"Turn around," Lilith said suddenly, turning off her screen. "I need to pee."

Michael looked at her in confusion.

"Turn around," she said again. "I'm not peeing with you watching me like that."

"You're wearing a suit. All you have to do—"

"I know what I have to do," she said, exasperated. "Now please turn around."

Michael sighed and faced away from her. "Okay, you can turn back now," she said after a minute. "That was the grossest thing ever."

"You should drink some energy gel."

"I'm not thirsty. Or hungry. Or whatever it is you have to be to drink that stuff."

"Drink it anyway. You need—"

"What I *need* is for you to stop telling me what to do!" she snapped.

Michael fumed. Why was she being such a brat? Did she think all of this was his fault? It wasn't like he could have known what would happen. They didn't even know what *had* happened. An accident, Randall had said, but that could mean anything. Maybe the station had just lost power, or maybe some critical circuit had gotten fried.

Or maybe it was much worse than that. He tried not to think about the possibilities.

Noon came and went. Michael called out again on the emergency channel, but all he got was static. Meanwhile, the magnetic field showed no signs that it was coming back, and the radiation from the flare was as strong as ever. He drank one of the bulbs of energy gel. It helped quiet the growling in his stomach, but it couldn't replace an actual full belly.

After a few more hours, Lilith stood up and stretched her arms above her head. "I'm tired of waiting. I'm going to explore."

"Explore what?" Michael asked.

"This cave," she said. "Maybe it leads somewhere."

"We need to stay here," Michael said. "This is where my dad will be searching for us."

"You don't know that," Lilith said. "All we know is that there was an accident at the station. Your dad and everyone else—"

She stopped suddenly.

"What?" Michael asked. "My dad and everyone else *what*?"

"Nothing. Never mind."

"Tell me!"

"Look, I'm just saying that maybe we can't sit here and wait for them to rescue us."

Michael narrowed his eyes. "You don't know what you're talking about."

"Whatever," Lilith said, shrugging. "Stay here if you want. I'm going to see where this cave leads."

She crouched down and began crawling into the narrow passage at the back of the cave. Michael glared at her. In just a moment she'd realize how stupid it was to go exploring in an ice-filled cave when all they had to do was sit here and wait for rescue.

A minute passed, and then two. After five minutes Michael sat up and peered toward the back of the cave.

"Lil?" he asked.

There was no response. He stood up and peered into the darkness. "Lilith?" he called again.

He tried to stay calm, but he couldn't help imagining all the possible things that could have happened to her. What if she'd been hurt? What if she'd slipped into a crevasse? He shouldn't have let her go alone. His heart raced as he scrambled along the icy floor of the cave. The passage turned to the right, cutting off the light from the cave entrance. Everything in front of him was pitch-black except for the narrow beam of his headlamp.

Cold sweat dripped down the back of his neck. She was somewhere down that passage, and she might need his help. He had to go after her, but his muscles were frozen in place. Raw, nameless terror gripped him.

"Lilith!" he tried to shout, but his breathing was so rapid and shallow that it was hardly more than a whisper.

He closed his eyes and clenched his fists, trying to stop them from trembling. What was he even afraid of? Why was he panicking like this? It wasn't the darkness, or the narrowness of the passage, or anything else he could name. He was just as scared of going backward as he was of going forward. His stomach cramped and he fought the urge to vomit.

His brain was going haywire, and he had to get it under control. He tried to remember what his doctor had taught him. His body, convinced that something terrible was just about to happen, was releasing massive amounts of adrenaline and cortisol, and now the fear center of his brain wanted to take over.

But the rest of his brain knew that this was just a cave and he wasn't in any real danger. All he had to do was crawl forward. Lilith had done it just because she wanted to explore. Now here he was, so petrified with fear that he couldn't follow her even when she needed his help?

He cocked his head to one side. Had it been his imagination, or had he just heard Lilith's voice? He listened intently. A moment later it came again: *Michael.*

She was calling for him. She needed his help. He couldn't stay here any longer. He scrambled forward frantically. The passage turned to the left and then back to the right. He went faster, ignoring the pain in his knees from the icy floor. Without any warning the tunnel bent sharply downward. His hands slipped out from under him and he started to slide. He tried to slow himself down by grabbing onto the walls on either side, but his fingers couldn't get a grip against the slick ice. He opened his mouth to scream.

Suddenly, the passage ended and he tumbled out onto a wide, flat area. He collided with something soft and rolled to a stop. His scream turned into a loud "oof."

"Nice entrance," Lilith said. Her voice was slightly muffled. "Very nimble. Now would you please get off me?"

"Lilith!" he gasped. "Are you okay?"

She climbed to her feet. "I'm fine. Except for some bruising where you decided to tackle me, anyway."

"I thought—I thought—"

He blinked sweat out of his eyes. His breathing was still rapid and his heart rate was elevated, but his body was going back to normal. It was as if the panic switch in his brain that had switched on back in the tunnel had just as suddenly been turned off.

"Didn't you hear me telling you to be careful?" Lilith asked. "The ice is wet and slippery down here."

Michael stood up and brushed ice and dirt off of his pants. He stopped and frowned. She was right: a thin layer of moisture covered the fabric of his suit. "There can't be liquid water here. The air is way too cold."

He checked the temperature. The air *should* have been way too cold. But his wrist display showed that it was five degrees above freezing. He wiped the screen with his thumb to make sure he was reading it right. Up on the surface, it had been seventy degrees below zero. Down here it should be even colder. What was going on?

"Come look at this," Lilith said.

He stood next to her and shone his headlamp around. They were inside a large natural cavern about twenty or thirty meters across. Stalactites of ice or rock were barely visible in the shadows above their heads. A few meters in front of them, the floor ended in a straight, sharp ledge that stretched from wall to wall.

They took a few cautious steps forward and peered down. The perfect ninety-degree angle of the ledge dropped ten meters down to a rock floor. On the far wall, at the bottom of the cave, a tunnel led deeper into the glacier. The ledge, the floor below, and the tunnel were all perfectly smooth, as if they'd been carved by a laser. Near the entrance to the tunnel, an ancient digging robot sat hunched over, glistening with a sheen of ice.

"This must be part of the old water-mining operation," Michael said.

Lilith nodded excitedly. "Which means that tunnel has to lead to the station."

"It *might* lead to the station," Michael said. He stared at the passageway uneasily. What if they got lost down here? What if one of them got hurt? What if he panicked again?

But maybe Lilith was right. If they just waited for help, they might be stuck here until the flare ended.

On one side, the ice had been cut away right up to

the rock wall of the cave. Lilith found handholds and footholds and started to descend. When she was almost to the ground, she jumped off the wall. Her boots kicked up a tiny splash of water as she landed. Michael jumped down next to her and they inspected the mining robot. Its head was bent as if it were sleeping. It had two long, straight, fingerless arms like the blades of a forklift.

"This guy hasn't been used in a long time," Lilith said.

Michael knelt down and examined the floor of the cave. Little rivulets of water were flowing through cracks and channels in the rock, eventually converging in a wide, shallow stream that flowed into the tunnel. He pressed his hand against the rock floor. Even through his gloves he could feel that it was warm.

Hypothesis: something was heating the rock below and melting the ice. But *what* was generating all of that heat? He couldn't come up with a single explanation that made any sense.

"There's no way this should be happening," he said.

"Shoulds and oughts and turkey trots," Lilith said. "That's something my aunt used to say. It means—"

"I get what it means." He followed the tiny streams of water until they converged into a wide, shallow pool around the mining robot's feet and then flowed out of the cave and down the tunnel.

"Where is all the water going?" Lilith asked. "I mean,

it has to go somewhere, right?"

"I think we should find out."

They started down the tunnel. For a hundred meters or so, the passage was straight and almost level, and the water was only deep enough to make a quiet, rhythmic splashing as they walked. Soon the tunnel met up with a wider passage, and the water grew deeper. After a few dozen meters it was running around their ankles in a strong current, and Michael's legs were getting tired from the effort of sloshing ahead.

How far would it be to the station? The glacier was a kilometer or so across. They'd come about half that distance so far, but was it in the right direction?

"Do you hear that?" Lilith asked. "It sounds like the ocean."

Michael listened. She was right. What he'd thought was just static from his radio was clearly the sound of rushing water. After a couple of minutes, the sound was noticeably louder and the water at their feet had risen another twenty centimeters. Abruptly, the tunnel opened up into another large cavern. They stood at the opening of a new cave and looked around.

This cave was much wider than the previous one, with a dome-shaped roof that was at least seventy or eighty meters across. Even with their headlamps turned up to their most powerful settings, they couldn't see the far wall. It seemed to be a nexus or hub, with several other tunnels converging on this one spot. The floor was covered in a knee-deep pool of water that was being fed by streams from the various tunnels. Chunks of ice floated in the pool, some as big as small houses. Water plunged out of a meter-wide gap near the center of the ceiling, churning the pool into a white froth.

"The whole glacier is melting," Michael said. He still didn't understand what was happening, but the more he saw, the more worried he got.

"We already know there's nothing back the way we came," Lilith said. "One of these tunnels must lead to the station. We just have to figure out which one. Don't you have a compass or anything?"

"The magnetic field failed, remember? I can't . . ."

He trailed off. The *planetary* magnetic field had failed. But somewhere nearby, underneath the station, was one of the inducers: a massive, quantum-entangled electromagnet. Were they close enough for the inducer itself to attract a compass?

With a loud *crack*, a piece of ice in the ceiling broke away and collapsed into the pool of water. Lilith grabbed onto Michael, and they braced themselves against the waist-high waves that sloshed all around. The gap in the ceiling was now almost two meters wide, and water was pouring out in a gigantic white column.

"Wherever we're going, we need to go fast," Lilith shouted over the roar of the water.

He pulled up the navigation display on his wrist unit. The compass needle swiveled aimlessly. For a moment it swung toward his left and held still before wandering around again. Michael sloshed through the water toward a tunnel on the left side of the cavern, and the needle snapped into place. He turned around completely, but the needle remained pointing at the left-hand tunnel no matter which way he faced.

"That way," he said. "I think."

Lilith splashed past him and took a few steps into the tunnel. Like the other passages, it was man-made and perfectly straight, but with a noticeable upward slope. An ankle-deep stream of water flowed down into the pool they were standing in.

Another chunk of ice collapsed into the pool. "Come on," Lilith said, grabbing his arm and pulling him into the tunnel.

The beams of their headlamps stretched out into the darkness ahead. The water flowing back down toward the cave sucked at their boots, adding effort to each step. After a few minutes Michael's legs were aching, but there was still no sign of another cave or even a bend in the passage. He stopped, breathing heavily, and leaned against the wall.

"How far have we come?" Lilith asked, shining her light back down the tunnel.

"I don't know," Michael panted, wishing he had Earth-born muscles like her. She'd hardly broken a sweat. "Maybe a hundred—"

The floor under their feet rumbled briefly. They glanced at each other and, without saying a word, started climbing again. Michael's legs screamed in protest but he pushed himself onward.

From somewhere behind them came a deep, echoing boom, and a moment later a strong gust of air rushed past them. Michael stumbled and Lilith grabbed his arm to keep him from falling.

"Keep going!" Lilith shouted. Michael's lungs burned as they scrambled through the tunnel. Was it growing smaller, tighter, steeper? There was no space around him, nowhere to move, nothing to breathe . . .

Suddenly the passage emptied out into another natural cave. Michael put his hands on his knees and gasped for air. This room was smaller than the last, and it had only two tunnels intersecting it. A rusted forklift sat against one wall next to a pile of crates. He checked his compass. This time it pointed toward the tunnel on the opposite side of the room without hesitation.

"We're getting closer," he gasped.

They jogged up the far tunnel. The water surged

around their calves. Michael shone his light up the passage. They were climbing higher—how was the water getting deeper? Was there another flooded room ahead of them?

He turned around and looked back they way they'd come. Somehow, the water behind them was rising. But how was that possible?

The pieces of the puzzle clicked together in his mind, and immediately that familiar black terror rose up again. He could suddenly picture the immense weight of the glacier pressing down all around them as its lower levels slowly melted and collapsed, driving the water lever higher and higher until it had filled every possible space. . . .

"Run!" he shouted.

But running was impossible. The water was almost up to their knees now, and all they could do was slosh forward as quickly as they could. The muscles in Michael's legs threatened to cramp, but he pushed himself on. Ten meters, twenty meters . . .

Then the passage ended so abruptly that Michael had to put his hands out to keep from smacking into the wall. It was flat and smooth, like someone had sealed the tunnel off.

No, he thought. *It can't end like this.*

Lilith looked around frantically. The beam of her headlamp reflected off something metallic on the side of the tunnel. She sloshed over to the wall and opened a small panel, revealing a row of buttons and pressure gauges. Michael and Lilith froze for a moment, both suddenly realizing what they were looking at: the control systems for an airlock.

Lilith smacked the green cycle button with her fist. The flat wall in front of them split in two and started to slide open. Water poured through the gap into the airlock. But when the door had opened only about twenty centimeters, the control panel on the wall erupted in a shower of sparks, and the door shuddered and stopped.

Michael and Lilith pulled at the door futilely with their fingers. Michael turned himself sideways and tried to squeeze inside, but his helmet was too wide to fit through the gap. Lilith jabbed the buttons on the control panel frantically. Behind them, the sound of the rising water was a dull roar that grew louder and louder with each passing second.

Michael stretched his arm through the door and tried to reach the control panel on the far wall of the airlock, but his fingers clawed at empty air. A large chunk of ice struck the airlock door next to him and splintered into a dozen smaller fragments.

"We have to get this door open!" Lilith shouted.

Michael's eyes latched onto the pressure gauge in the airlock, which was showing twenty thousand pascals—

almost five times higher than normal for Mars's thin atmosphere. Could that be correct? He checked his wrist display, but it gave the same reading.

Hypothesis, he thought suddenly. *The rising water is pushing the air into a smaller and smaller space, causing the pressure to rise.* And if that was the case, then he knew how he could get inside the airlock.

"I'm going to take off my helmet!" he yelled.

Lilith's mouth hung open. "You're going to do *what?*"

Michael double-checked his calculations. Twenty thousand pascals was dangerous, but it wasn't deadly. Without his helmet, he'd be able to squeeze through the gap in the doors. As long as he could hold his breath long enough to get the airlock working again, he'd survive.

And if he couldn't, they were dead anyway.

His first problem was how to remove his helmet. He couldn't just yank it off and climb through. His suit was set to seventy thousand pascals, and the sudden drop in pressure would be like a bomb going off. He turned the manual-release valve on his collar until he could hear the hiss of air escaping. His ears popped and a warning light flashed on the inside of his helmet. He ignored it and opened the valve farther. His suit tightened around his body as the air inside bled out into the tunnel.

"Whatever you're doing, do it fast," Lilith pleaded.

She was right—the water was up to their waists, and

he didn't have time to make this slow and easy. He opened the valve another half turn. When the pressure in his suit had reached thirty thousand pascals, he pulled the release lever on his collar.

There was a loud *whoosh* as the rest of the air in his suit rushed out all at once. His ears exploded in pain. He yanked off his helmet and shoved it into Lilith's hands and slipped through the opening in the doors. He found the override switch on the airlock control panel and jerked it downward.

The doors slid open. Water flooded into the airlock, sweeping Lilith inside. Michael sagged against the wall, his lungs screaming for oxygen. Lilith slid his helmet over his head, and he fumbled to clasp it shut. She pushed his hands out of the way and snapped it into his collar. Immediately he felt a cool rush of air against his face as his suit began to repressurize.

"Close it," he gasped, pointing at the panel.

Lilith pressed a button on the control panel, and the door started to slide shut. With a loud crash, a person-sized slab of ice crashed against the airlock and wedged itself in the gap between the door and the frame. The door ground against the ice for a moment, and then it stopped.

"Push!" Lilith shouted. Her voice was faint and far-off. She threw herself against the ice, but her feet couldn't get any traction. Michael put his feet against the wall and pressed his back against hers. Together they pushed the chunk of ice back a few centimeters, and then a few more. With a loud *crack*, the ice broke into two pieces and slipped out into the passage. A moment later the doors slid shut.

Outside, more chunks of ice crashed against the airlock door. The sound of the rushing water rose in pitch until the tunnel filled completely and everything was silent. Michael blinked and shook his head, trying get his senses to return to normal.

He pushed the button to start the airlock cycle and open the inner doors. The control panel beeped and flashed an error message. Michael stared at the display in shock.

"No," Lilith said. "No, no, no. Don't tell me the airlock isn't working."

"The airlock is fine," he said. "But . . . there's no air on the other side."

"What do you mean? How could there not be any air?"

Michael swallowed hard. "The station had a pressure breach."

8

"PRESSURE BREACH?" LILITH repeated.

Quickly, Michael searched for the override command on the control panel. The inner doors slid open and water flooded out in a long cascade, revealing a long, dimly lit corridor. Shards of glass from the overhead light bars littered the floor. Reddish-brown dust hung in thick, motionless clouds On the wall next to the airlock was a poster of a suited woman with the caption Safety First.

This wasn't an accident. It was a disaster.

Lilith saw the expression on his face. "Don't worry. I'm sure everyone is fine."

He nodded almost imperceptibly, and they stepped out into the hallway. In the dust-filled air, the beams from their headlamps seemed solid enough to touch. The first doorway opened onto an airlock prep room. Most of the suits were gone from the walls, and a box of emergency supplies had been pulled out and dumped onto the floor. The second room was filled with a jumble of equipment, some of it clearly left over from the station's water-mining days: rope, jackhammers, drills, fusion torches. A cart filled with wires, clamps, and diagnostic equipment bore a hand-lettered sign: Personal Property of James Lee.

They followed the corridor down to a large room that had been carved from solid rock. At the far end of the room, a gigantic floor-to-ceiling window looked out onto the plains below. The glass from the window had been shattered, and clouds of dust blew in through the opening. Stairways ran up to a second floor and down into a basement area, and two other corridors like the one they'd come through led back into the ice cap. In the center of the room was a long plastic table, some chairs, and an L-shaped couch. The chairs and table had been knocked over, and dishes were scattered over the floor. A thin layer of red dust covered everything in sight.

Michael felt dizzy. He recognized this as the station's common area. Sometimes when his dad called, he would be sitting on that couch or leaning against the window. There were always people visible in the background, talking and working and laughing. Now it looked . . . dead.

Lilith stepped carefully across the broken glass and inspected the shattered window. Outside, the sun was close to setting, and the craggy surface of the northern plains glowed like a blood-red sea. Michael stood in the shadow of the window frame and peered down. Ten meters below was a narrow path that was barely big enough for a rover. Past that, a steep drop led to a crevasse where glittering white ice from the glacier wound back and forth like a frozen river.

"I don't get it," Lilith said. "What could have done this? It's like a bomb went off in the middle of the station."

Michel picked up a small fragment of window. It was old-fashioned plexiglass, not transplastic, but still, it would have taken a lot of force to shatter it like this. Lilith was right—something had exploded.

But what?

"I don't know," Michael said, pulling at her arm. "But stay out of the sunlight as much as you can."

"Right," Lilith said, stepping away from the window. "Lethal radiation and all that."

They split up and each searched one of the two wings of the lower level.

Michael found a laboratory that looked like it hadn't been used in years along with a couple of storage rooms filled with food and other supplies. At the end of the corridor was another airlock like the one they'd come through. Its gauge showed extremely high air pressure on the other side. *Because it's not air,* he thought. *It's water.* All of the tunnels that led into the glacier had probably flooded by now.

Lilith met him as he ran back to the hub. "I found the kitchen," she said. "Some jars of spaghetti sauce burst. I thought it was blood."

The dishes on the floor of the common area rattled as a tremor ran through the station. Lilith looked at Michael worriedly. "I don't like this."

On the second floor they found three more corridors and a communal bath area. Water dripped from one of the showerheads, and shreds of toilet paper were scattered everywhere. Lilith poked her head into the first doorway in one of the corridors. She gasped.

"Bodies."

Michael pushed past her. The room was a small clinic. The floors and walls were all painted white, and there was a raised operating table in the middle of the room. Two beds with privacy curtains sat against one wall. On the opposite side of the room, a white sheet had been laid out. Four bodies, two men and two women, were lying on the sheet. Their faces were blue and covered with a thin layer of frost.

Michael's heart stopped. Neither of the men was his father, but he kept looking back and forth between them as if he were worried that one of their faces might morph into his dad's at any moment. His knees felt weak.

"Did you know any of them?" Lilith asked, visibly shaken.

Michael pointed at one of the women. "I met her once at my dad's office in Heimdall," he said hoarsely. "She helped me with a calculus problem."

"I'm sorry," Lilith said.

Michael fought a sudden urge to vomit. Lilith shouldn't be apologizing to him. He couldn't even remember the woman's name. He didn't know the other people at all. And right now the only feeling he could summon was relief that none of them was his father. They deserved better. His hands trembling, he found a second white sheet and laid it out over them. It wasn't much, but it was something.

"Whatever happened, it didn't happen in here," Lilith said. "Someone must have brought them here after the accident. Who was that? And where are they now?"

They walked up and down the corridors on the second level, inspecting each room briefly. Everywhere they looked, they found signs that whoever had been here had left in a hurry. A screen in one office had been left on, and in the next room down they found a half-eaten cookie. Michael racked his brain to figure out what could have happened, but he couldn't come up with a rational explanation.

"Michael," Lilith said, pausing in one of the doorways. "You need to see this."

Inside was a desk with a keyboard and screen, sitting

in front of a window that looked out onto the slope of the glacier. In the center of the room, a chair for visitors lay on its side. A few pieces of paper with what looked like geometric calculations sat on the desk, along with a framed photo showing Michael and Peter in the neighborhood swimming pool.

"This was my dad's office," Michael said.

Was. Because his dad had left. He'd evacuated with the others, hours ago, and now all that was left in the station were corpses.

Ever since the magnetic field had failed, Michael had been convinced that all they needed to do was get here and everything would be okay. He'd been sure that his dad was looking for him. But now . . . they were alone.

Numbly, Michael picked up one of the pieces of paper from the desk. It looked like a basic trigonometry problem. Why had his dad been working on this? And why had he been doing it by hand, instead of using his screen? Michael looked at the problem, and its answer appeared in his head, almost unbidden. *Congratulations,* he told himself. *You can solve trigonometry problems in your head. Too bad you don't have any* useful *skills.*

The floor rumbled again. Lilith put her hand on his arm. "Michael . . ."

"Do you know my dad's favorite thing to talk about?" he asked. "*Someday.* It's like it's the only thing he thinks about. Someday I'll be cured. Someday I'll go outside with him again. Someday I'll go into the Service, like him.

"Except I'm probably *never* going to be cured, because lots of times, suit anxiety doesn't go away completely. Did you know that?"

"That's what I've heard," Lilith said quietly.

"So why won't he ever talk about what I can do *now*? Why won't he talk about what I'll do if I never stop having panic attacks?"

"I don't know," she said. "Maybe he's trying to encourage you. Or maybe he's scared. Or maybe he's just a complete and total idiot."

Michael snorted. "Maybe."

"Trust me," she said. "I've had a lot of experience in the idiotic dad department. Want to hear a story?"

"Sure," Michael said, surprised.

"Have you ever heard of the Florida Keys?"

Michael shook his head.

"They're islands not too far from Miami, close to where my dad lives. When I was a kid, he promised me someday we'd take his boat and go sailing there, just the two of us. But every summer, there was some reason why we couldn't go. He was too busy at work, or there was going to be a hurricane, or whatever.

"So when I tell my dad that my mom and I are going

to move to Mars, he gets all excited. He shows me these articles about the big lake in the Hesperia colony, where apparently you can actually sail a boat."

"I've heard about that," Michael said.

"He says that he's going to come visit and take me sailing. He says that maybe he'll even move here permanently. But for months, he keeps having all these problems with his visa. He complains about how complicated they make it, how you have to supply all these forms, how they keep rejecting him for stupid things.

"A few weeks ago, I decide to surprise him by doing the application myself. I'm going to finish all the paperwork so that he can come here this summer. So I spend hours filling out all of his information, and then finally I get back a response that I've entered the wrong home address.

"I think, that's stupid, there's no way I got that address wrong. I went there every weekend for five years, right? So I do a little research. Apparently there's a lot you can look up, even from two hundred million kilometers away. Like, for example, you can find out that last year your dad got remarried and moved in with some other woman and her kids, and he never even bothered to tell you."

Michael raised his eyebrows. "Seriously?"

"Well, that's the thing, right? It seemed too crazy to be true. I'm thinking, maybe there was just some mix-up with someone else with the same name. So like an idiot,

I go looking for photos. It doesn't take long to find them, including a great one of him and his new bratty-looking kids, sailing his boat down in the Florida Keys."

"Wow."

"Even after all that, I still wasn't convinced. I needed to hear him say it, I guess. So the other day when he called, I asked him about it."

"The other day?" Michael asked. "You mean, when I came over to your house?"

"Yeah," Lilith said. "Feels like forever ago, doesn't it? I showed him the photos, and finally he admitted that it's all true. He's married, he's got stepkids, and they go sailing all the time. And the best part? He actually never even *started* his visa application. Everything about that had been a lie from day one.

"My mom is furious. She wants to go back there, show up at his new house, and punch him in the face. I'm mad, but you know what's funny? I'm not mad at him.

"I'm mad at *myself*—because some silly eight-year-old-girl part of me still thinks someday he's going to show up here and say, 'Hey, sweetie, let's go sailing.'"

She clenched her jaw tightly and stared down at the floor. Not knowing what else to do, Michael reached out and squeezed her hand. "I don't think that's silly."

"Yeah, well, I guess we're both pretty stupid then."

The desk rattled as another tremor ran through the station. Lilith straightened up and took a deep breath. Suddenly, except for an almost imperceptible hoarseness in her voice, she was back to her usual, imperturbable self. "As much as I love reminiscing about idiotic fathers . . ."

"I know," he said. "Let's go."

9

"SO I FIGURE that if we're going to get out of here, we need to find an exit that isn't blocked by umpteen million liters of water," Lilith said. "And the lower floor is the only place we haven't looked."

As they climbed down the stairs to the basement level, the air grew noticeably warmer. The stairwell led to a large tunnel that had been bored out of solid rock. Just to their right was a cargo airlock that led back into the glacier. An error light on its control panel showed that the other side was filled with water, just like the other airlocks they'd found.

Without saying anything, they made their way down the tunnel until it ended in a room that was a cross between a garage and a laboratory. On one side of the room was a large set of doors that were slightly open, leaving a narrow gap that let in a gleam of reddish light from the setting sun. Tools and wrecked equipment were everywhere, and the floor was covered with glass and bits of debris. In the center of the room was a metal shaft about three meters across that descended into the rocky floor. The air above the shaft quivered and shimmered with heat.

"This is the magnetic inducer," Michael said.

"I think you mean it *was* the magnetic inducer," Lilith said, looking around at the wreckage. She stood near the shaft and peered down. "So this thing reaches all the way through the planet?"

"It only goes down a few kilometers. There's a—"

"Weird quantum reaction with the other one at the south pole," Lilith finished. "I remember now."

"I don't understand what happened," Michael said, picking up a bit of debris. "Something obviously exploded. But what? Why aren't there any signs of a fire?"

"Does it really matter?" Lilith said. She flipped the switch that controlled the outer doors, but nothing happened. She picked up a long metal bar and wedged one end into the narrow gap between the doors.

"Well, why did everyone evacuate, then? Once the

station depressurized, the worst danger was over. Why didn't they try to repair the damage?"

"Maybe they were just lazy," Lilith grunted, pulling at the metal bar. "Dunno. Can you give me a hand?"

Michael imagined his father standing here a few hours ago, surveying the damage. As the officer in charge, he must have been the one to make the decision to evacuate. But why? What was he afraid of?

His eyes fell on a desk screen that lay on the floor. He picked it up and set it back on a nearby table. The screen displayed a series of temperature measurements taken at one-minute intervals. Most of the values hovered around minus seventy. He scrolled back further, and the temperature readings spiked up sharply, going from freezing to boiling and then dropping back down again.

His heart beat faster. Someone had been monitoring this data right before they decided to leave, so clearly it was important. But *what* was it measuring?

The display refreshed and added another point to the graph. He blinked in surprise. The data was still being collected. He traced his finger down the last few readings. They quickly climbed from minus seventy to minus thirty, minus ten, and ended with the latest point: five degrees above freezing.

Lilith repositioned the metal bar and yanked on it with both hands. She'd managed to open up a gap about twenty centimeters wide. "Could really use some help here," she growled.

Sweat trickled down Michael's neck. It was getting uncomfortably warm in his suit.

Warm. Suddenly it all made sense. The melting of the glacier. The "explosion" at the station. The evacuation afterward. Michael pulled up the temperature reading on his wrist display. Five degrees above freezing—the same as the last point on the graph.

The screen was monitoring the air temperature *in this room.*

He looked up at Lilith. "We have to get out of here!" he said. "Now!"

"What do you think I'm trying to do?" she snapped. She tried to squeeze herself through the gap in the doors, but it was still too narrow.

A cloud of steam and water vapor began to rise out of the shaft. Michael could feel the sudden heat, even through the insulation in his suit. He grabbed Lilith's arm.

"We don't have time!" he said, pointing at the shaft. "It's happening all over again. We have to get out *now*!"

When the inducers had failed, they hadn't just turned to dormant pieces of metal. They were still reacting with the energy from the flare, and without anywhere else to go, that energy was being turned into heat. Far below the station, that heat was turning ice to water and then to steam. Just like earlier this morning, the pressure from the steam was rising to unimaginable levels. And just like then, it would soon reach a breaking point, and the steam would explode through the only route available: the shaft of the magnetic inducer itself.

That was why his father had evacuated the station. Not because of the first explosion. Because of the *second* explosion that they knew would be coming.

The floor of the cargo bay trembled violently. Water vapor poured out of the shaft and spilled across the floor like smoke. A low roaring sound came from the depths of the shaft, growing louder and louder with every second.

Something seemed to click in Lilith's mind. "Go!" she shouted, dropping the metal bar and pushing him toward the door.

Side by side they sprinted along the corridor, dodging past scattered piles of equipment and debris. There was a high-pitched squeal as a cloud of steam burst through the cargo bay doors and into the passage, scalding their backs and shoulders. They ran up the stairwell and into the common area. The superheated air swept past them and out through the shattered window with such force that they had to grab one of the support columns to keep from being knocked over.

Michael looked out over the edge of the shattered window. Ten meters below him, a small footpath had been carved into the side of the cliff. But to get there, they'd need to climb down a near-vertical rock wall. He clutched the windowsill so hard his hand started to cramp. Everything around the ice cap seemed to be expanding, like a scene printed on a sheet of rubber that was being pulled in all directions. The horizon spread out, farther and farther, until Michael was just a tiny speck of dust floating in an infinite nothingness. He dropped down to the floor, hardly noticing the shards of plexiglass that pressed painfully against his knees.

I can't do it

The wind roared around him. His grip on the edge of the window loosened. The yawning void in front of him seemed to be pulling him forward.

I can't

The nothingness called him: let go, drift away, be swallowed up. There was no point in fighting anymore.

do it

"Yes, you can," Lilith said, grabbing him by the shoulders. "Michael—look at me!"

She was shouting at him, but her voice was soft and

far-off, like a tiny light flashing in darkness. "I'm right here! You're okay. But we have to climb down. Do you understand?"

His eyes focused on her, and the world snapped back into place. The wind roared and the floor of the station trembled. Pieces of plexiglass rattled and slid off the edge and tumbled down the mountainside.

"I'll give you one guess," she said.

He stared at her in confusion. One guess?

"About which girl has a crush on you." Her voice was casual, as if this were the most normal thing in the world to bring up right now. She helped him lie down on his stomach and slide out toward the edge. "That's it. There are lots of footholds. It's an easy climb."

Michael knew she was lying, but he willed himself to believe her. He slid his feet out and felt for the spot where the outside wall of the station met the rocky slope. Inch by inch he lowered himself until only his fingertips were clutching the ledge. He angled his head and tried to look down, but she grabbed his arm.

"Don't look!" she shouted. "Now are you going to make that guess, or what?"

Was she actually talking about this right now? He needed to focus on the slope in front of him and the yawning void below him, both of which were infinitely more important right now than middle school crushes.

But like a muscle twitching in reflex, his brain called up a name from his class.

"Gwen Mackenzie?" he heard himself say.

Lilith helped him put one foot into a crevice a half meter down the slope, and they both found new handholds. When they were secure again, she leaned toward him and shouted into his ear. "Gwen Mackenzie has as much personality as a two-by-four!"

"I guess," he said. "But she's got a nice smile."

"You'd be better off kissing a poodle!" With graceful agility, she climbed down a little lower and helped him find another foothold.

Over and over they repeated the process: stretch a foot downward, find a new spot, rest and reset. Each time Michael found a new handhold, he told himself that it didn't matter how far he'd come or how far he still had to go—right here, right at this spot, he was safe. He kept his mind focused on the mechanics of climbing and tried not to think about the vast emptiness surrounding him. A step, and then another step, over and over, like a dance in slow motion, until the footpath was only a few meters below them.

"That's it," she said. "We're almost there. Just keep going like this, and—"

There was an enormous *bang* like a thunderclap, and a moment later a blast of superheated air rushed over their heads. The wind howled, clawing at them with a million tiny fingers. Michael tried to grab a nearby rock with one hand, but it tore loose from the mountainside and he tumbled downward. He hit the ground hard, the impact knocking the wind from his lungs like a punch to the gut. Lilith landed beside him and rolled toward the edge of the path. Michael reached out reflexively and caught the shoulder strap of her air vest. Her legs swung out into the empty air and she dangled there, her fingers scrabbling for a handhold in the dirt. Michael heaved backward and pulled her up slowly, until finally she collapsed on the trail next to him.

"Thanks," she gasped.

He nodded. "You too."

The wind roared around them, pushing them in every direction. They held hands and walked along the narrow path. Twice Michael lost his footing and might have fallen if Lilith hadn't been there. The sunlight had faded to almost nothing, making it hard to see more than a few meters in any direction. A near-constant rumbling came from deep within the ice cap, and rocks and debris tumbled past them every few seconds.

Finally the footpath merged with a much wider, rutted roadway. After a hundred meters, it flattened out and started to wind through the hills and valleys at the base of the ice cap. Several times Michael stumbled with exhaustion, but he pressed on, determined to get as far away from the ruined magnetic field station as possible.

"Did you see that?" Lilith asked, jerking to a halt. "A light—over there!"

Michael squinted in the direction she was pointing, but all he saw was darkness and dust. "I don't see anything."

"There's something there!" she insisted. "I saw it!"

He paused. It was safest to stay on this roadway. If they got lost in the darkness, it might be impossible to find their way back. And the solar flare was going on, which meant they had to find some kind of shelter before sunrise. But if Lilith really had seen a light . . .

He let her half lead, half drag him off of the path and down a shallow slope. They jogged through the darkness, weaving around rocks and gullies that might trip them up or break an ankle. Michael was just about to tell Lilith that they needed to turn around when he saw a gleam of light somewhere ahead. He angled his headlamp, revealing a set of airlock doors built into the side of a dome-shaped hillock.

They exchanged an excited look and ran toward the airlock. The doors were heavy and primitive, with two small windows that were so yellowed with age that it was impossible to see through them. Maybe this was where his father and the rest of the research station had evacuated to! Michael pressed the button, and the doors slid open. The airlock was tiny, barely large enough for the two of them. Lilith started the cycle, and air pumps in the ceiling chugged.

As soon as the inner doors slid open, Michael tore his helmet off and rushed out into a T-shaped intersection with hallways on either side. The only light came from a few emergency lamps in the walls. Red dust covered everything. The air was bitterly cold, with a harsh, metallic taste, and his breath puffed out in little white clouds.

"Hello?" Michael shouted. "Is anyone here?"

He ran down one of the hallways and reached a small kitchen with an attached eating area. A metal countertop divided the room in two. On the far side were a sink, some cabinets, and a grease-stained stove. There were no windows, and the only functioning light in the ceiling buzzed and flickered continually. A man wearing a suit without a helmet sat at a table on the other side of the counter with his leg propped up on a chair. His face had a day's worth of grayish stubble, and he looked as exhausted as Michael felt, but he was instantly recognizable.

"Randall!" Michael blurted out.

Randall looked up at them. He blinked for a moment, as if he wasn't sure what he was seeing, and then he exhaled slowly. "I thought I was hearing things," he murmured.

"Are you okay?" Michael asked, moving around the countertop toward the table. Randall's leg was wrapped in a white sheet. Small red spots were visible along his thigh where blood had soaked through.

"I'll be okay," he said. "I'm alive, which is better off than I thought I'd be twelve hours ago."

Lilith peered down the hallway on the other side of the eating area. Everything was dark and quiet. "Where is everyone else?"

Randall shook his head. "There is no everyone else. We're the only ones here."

10

MICHAEL STARED AT him. "What are you talking about?" he asked. "Where is everyone? Where is my dad?"

"At Milankovic Station, I assume," Randall said. "That's the rendezvous point for an evacuation. I was holed up in a cave most of the day. I only made it here a little while before you did."

"Wait," Lilith said. "What do you mean, you assume? Didn't you talk to them?"

"I couldn't get a signal through," Randall said. "The interference was too heavy."

Michael's mouth fell open. If Randall hadn't been in contact with anyone at the station, then his dad didn't even know they were *here.*

Randall read Michael's expression. "Please tell me you told someone back home where you were going? Left a note, or something?"

Michael and Lilith looked at each other. "My brother knows we went outside," Michael said heavily. "But not that we were coming here."

"You drove out to the station, on your own, and didn't tell a single person?"

"It was kind of a last-minute decision," Lilith said.

Randall exhaled slowly. "Well, that complicates things."

"They know you're here, right?" Michael asked. "Won't someone be coming back to search for you?"

"Yes and no," Randall said. "The good news is that this is probably one of the first places they'll look."

"What's the bad news?" Lilith asked.

"The bad news is that it may be a while before they even get the chance to look. Days, at least, and maybe weeks. This is a planetwide emergency, and the Rescue Service has got their hands full right now. Looking for me isn't going to be high on their list."

"Oh, that's just *fantastic*," Lilith said, leaning her head against the wall.

"Count your blessings. You're lucky to be alive. Now, first—are either of you hurt?"

Lilith flexed her shoulder. "Just sore."

"All right," Randall said. "There are some supplies in the kitchen. Let me see if I can whip up some dinner."

"I'll eat anything as long as it isn't energy gel," Lilith said. "But I'll love you forever if you tell me there's a working bathroom in this place."

"Right over there," Randall said, pointing. He stood up with some difficulty and hobbled into the kitchen area.

"I can make dinner," Michael offered.

"Moving around is probably good for me," Randall said. "I don't want it to stiffen up too much. But if you want to help, grab that pot."

Lilith opened the door Randall had pointed to. "All I have to say is: between real food and a working toilet, I think I'm in heaven." She wrinkled her nose. "On the other hand, bathrooms in heaven probably don't smell like someone died in them."

After a quick inventory of the cabinets and some experimentation with the ancient-looking stove, Michael and Randall set out three cups of water and three steaming bowls of vegetable curry with rice. "No utensils, unfortunately, but now's not the time to stand on manners."

They slurped directly from the bowls, getting curry all over their chins and noses in the process. It tasted bland and a little sour, and Michael guessed that it had probably passed its shelf life at least a decade ago, but at least it was real food. As soon as he took the first bite, his stomach knotted with hunger, as if it had just realized that he hadn't eaten anything solid in over a day. He gulped the rest down as quickly as he could.

"So what is this place?" Lilith asked through a mouthful of curry.

"It's an old homestead," Randall said. "It was built back in the seventies, right after they started allowing families to stake claims and build private stations. It's been abandoned for ten or twenty years, I'd say."

"I can't believe people used to live like this." She arched her neck and looked around at the cramped kitchen area. Michael had to agree—it was a far cry from the homes in Heimdall. It was strange to imagine people spending almost all of their lives underground. But of course, until the magnetic field inducers had been built, this was how everyone had lived.

"It was in better shape back then, I imagine," Randall said. "The solar panels are working, more or less, but the battery won't hold much more than a day's charge. There's fresh water, and food for a week or two depending on how we stretch it out."

"But we're not going to just sit around waiting for someone to find us, are we?" Michael asked.

"We don't have any other options. It would take days to walk to Milankovic. And with this flare going on, we wouldn't make it thirty minutes once the sun came up."

He was right, of course. But Michael hated the idea of just sitting here. There had to be *something* they could do. If they couldn't get all the way to a colony, then maybe they could broadcast some sort of signal?

"So *now* you're all eager to go get help?" Lilith said. "When we're here, with food and water and a toilet? All I can say is that it's good one of us was smart enough to explore, instead of sitting around in that cave all day."

Michael frowned. "It was logical to stay put and wait for help. Just because it turned out that—"

"Oh, stupid me," Lilith said, throwing up her hands. "Expecting Michael Prasad to admit that he was wrong. I may as well wait for the next ice age."

"Cut it out," Randall said. "You're here, and that's what matters. Right now I think what we all need is some sleep. Maybe we can figure out a better plan in the morning."

Michael glared at Lilith as he took the bowls over to the sink. He was perfectly capable of admitting when he was wrong. And right now, he definitely didn't need her *gloating* like that.

After they'd cleaned up, Randall showed them to a small room in the back of the homestead. Without any windows, the room felt more like a storage closet than a bedroom. The antiquated airbeds wouldn't inflate, so they collected all the blankets they could find and spread them out on the floor.

"Can we take off our suits?" Lilith asked.

"Best to leave them on, just in case," Randall said. "We may need to leave in a hurry."

They removed their wrist screens and air units and lay down on the blankets. The floor was like ice, and Michael was glad for the heating elements in his suit.

"Good night," he said to Lilith, turning off the lights.

She pulled her blanket over her shoulders. "Night," she mumbled.

Michael couldn't tell if she was really already halfway asleep or just pretending to be so that she wouldn't have to talk to him. He lay on his back and looked up at the ceiling. But despite an exhaustion that seemed like it would swallow him whole, sleep didn't come quickly.

What was everyone in his family doing right now? Once the magnetic field failed, surely Peter would have told people that they had gone outside. He and their mom would have spent a panicked day huddled in an emergency shelter under the city, wondering what had happened to them. Now that the sun had gone down, there would be search parties looking for them. Would anyone be able to figure out where they had gone?

Did his dad even know they were missing? With communication satellites down, it might take a long time for information to go back and forth between the colonies.

He was probably busy orchestrating rescue efforts from Milankovic, believing that everyone back in Heimdall was safe.

And even if he did find out that they'd gone outside, the magnetic field station was probably the last place he would look. Nobody except Peter believed that Michael could stay out for more than a few minutes without freezing up. Even if he'd left a hand-painted sign telling them exactly where he was going, they probably would have just ignored it.

Michael rolled over and wrapped the blankets tightly around him. If they were lucky enough to survive all of this and make it back to Heimdall, nobody's opinion of him would change. They saw him the way they wanted to see him—like a kid with a *condition*. He could do somersaults on Phobos, and they'd still tell him that he ought to stay inside.

He had almost drifted off to sleep when Lilith spoke. "I can't *believe* you thought Gwen Mackenzie has a crush on you."

Michael sat up and rubbed his eyes. He looked around the room. Lilith was gone, and her makeshift pillow was sitting on the deflated airbed. He had a brief moment of panic before he heard her voice coming from the hallway. He reattached his wrist screen and squinted at the time . . . 1147. He'd slept till almost noon.

He walked blearily down to the common room. Lilith was sitting at the table and Randall was leaning against the counter, drinking a cup of coffee.

"Good morning," Lilith said.

Michael filled a cup with water from the sink and drank it down in quick gulps. "Morning," he said in a raspy voice.

"Want something to eat?" Randall asked. "Vegetable curry, breakfast of champions. There are even more boxes of it in the storage room down the hall there."

Michael wandered around for a few minutes until he found the storage room. Plastic boxes were stacked up haphazardly against the walls. A metal table with a bent leg sat in a corner, covered with tools and assorted junk. Something next to the table caught his eye: a fist-sized antenna. He pushed a few boxes and a ratty-looking chair out of the way and found an ancient-looking portable radio. Excitedly, he brushed off a layer of red dust and brought it into the common room.

"What's that?" Lilith asked.

"A radio!" Michael said. He set it down on the table and turned it on. The screen on the side blinked and came to life. It worked! Maybe they could use it to get a message to his dad.

Randall picked up the radio and inspected it. "Pretty

high-powered, looks like. Unfortunately, without any satellites it's not much use."

"Do you think it could reach Milankovic?" Michael asked.

"Sure," he said. "But Milankovic is over the horizon. A radio like this is only going to work if you've got line of sight."

"I don't understand," Lilith said. "My dad used to talk to ham radio operators who were thousands of kilometers away. Why can't we do that here?"

"Earth has an electrically charged layer in its atmosphere that can reflect signals over the horizon," Randall said. "Mars doesn't. That's why we we're so dependent on satellites."

"Oh," she said. "Drat."

Randall set the radio back down again. "But I'll bet we can set it up as a beacon, so that anyone who comes looking will know we're here."

Michael slumped back in his chair. Randall was right, of course. Basic geometry said that the curve of the Martian surface would put anything more than a few kilometers away out of sight.

He sucked in his breath. But basic geometry *also* said that the higher you were, the more of the planet you could see. He ran through some calculations in his head. Milankovic was a hundred kilometers away. Given the curvature of Mars, he'd have to find a spot that was thirteen hundred meters above the surface to have clear line of sight to the colony so he could get a signal to his dad.

And he knew exactly where that spot was.

11

"YOU SURE YOU want to do that?" Lilith asked, raising one eyebrow skeptically.

"I'm sure," Michael said.

"I'm just saying that maybe you should think it through a little more."

"I've thought it through," Michael insisted.

Lilith tossed her cards faceup on the table. "You've still got a lot to learn, mi amigo. Full house, tens over sevens."

Michael stared at her cards and then down at his own measly two pair. He grimaced. "This is a stupid game."

"Where'd you learn to play poker, anyway?" Randall asked, gathering the cards.

"Let me guess," Michael said. "Your dad taught you."

"Nope," Lilith said. "My mom. She used to take me to midstakes games in the offshore casinos. She says she'll give me my winnings when I turn eighteen."

"That's it—I'm out," Randall said. "And I'm starting to think that from now on we should play hearts."

"Oh, I'm even better at hearts," Lilith said. "But sure, whatever."

Randall looked at his wrist screen. "It should be dark by now. I've got a few things to check on outside, and then I'll make dinner."

Michael made a face. "Vegetable curry again?"

"Maybe there's a hidden supply room somewhere," Lilith said with a dreamy expression. "Filled with french fries, freeze-dried steaks, and orange soda."

"Could be," Randall said with a laugh. "You're free to look. Michael, do you want to help me set up that beacon?"

The one good thing about wearing your environment suit all day long was that it didn't take long to prep for going outside. As Michael slid his air vest over his head, Randall bent down and picked a piece of paper off the floor.

"What's this?" he asked, unfolding it. "Doing some calculations?"

It was the piece of paper from his dad's room in the station. Michael must have stuffed it into his pocket without thinking. He grabbed it from Randall and folded it back up. "It's just something I found. It's not important."

Randall cocked his head to one side. "If you say so."

Michael took a deep breath and snapped his helmet into place. His stomach churned with an all-too-familiar anxiety as he counted the seconds until the air unit started up. *One, two . . .*

"Here," Randall said, startling him. "Hold this."

He shoved a metal tripod into Michael's hands and picked up the radio and a plastic toolbox. "Ready?"

Michael did a quick check of his suit diagnostics and gave Randall a thumbs-up. They cycled through the airlock and stepped out onto the surface. The wind was still gusting back and forth angrily. The sun had set a little while ago, and the sky to the west was a sea of red and pink and orange. Randall checked his radiation monitor.

"We're good," he said, and set the radio on the ground.

Michael unfolded the tripod and positioned it a few meters from the airlock. A patch of dust swirled up into a cloud around his ankles and then settled back down again. The wind seemed to be coming steadily from the north, off the ice cap, which was unusual for this time of year. He craned his head back and squinted at the rocky cliff but couldn't see any sign of the station. Was there anything left after yesterday's explosion?

Randall detached the antenna and wedged it into the top of the tripod, with a thin wire running from the antenna to the base of the radio. "See if you can dig up a hex driver and a set of needle-nose pliers. This thing is an antique. Pretty sure we'll have to hard wire it."

Michael dug through the toolbox and handed him the tools. Randall knelt down and used the hex driver to open a panel on the back of the radio, exposing a circuit board and some multicolored wires.

"I've been meaning to ask you something," Randall said, peering into the guts of the radio. "When you took the suit test, what happened? Why did it take you so long to finish the navigation section? I thought you'd be the first one back."

"I didn't realize we were allowed to use our nav computer," Michael said. "I had to use a range finder and a compass to figure out where I was."

Randall squinted up at him. "And you did all of that in your *head*?"

"I'm pretty good at math," Michael said, shrugging.

"That piece of paper—it was in your dad's office, wasn't it?" Randall said. "Now I remember. When we got back from Heimdall, he asked me if I could work out my position using just a distance and angle to some point. I told him maybe, but only if I had a math textbook and a few hours."

Michael looked at the paper again. "I don't think he got it right, either."

Randall burst out laughing. "I'm not surprised. Your dad is a smart guy, but that sort of thing is exactly why we have nav computers. I'll bet ninety-nine out of a hundred Rescue Service officers couldn't manage it—and you did it without even using a calculator?"

"It's not *that* hard," Michael mumbled.

"Neither is rocket science. Wait . . . don't tell me—you're a whiz at rocket science too?"

"I know the basics," Michael said stiffly.

"I guess I shouldn't be surprised. Your dad talks all the time about what a genius you are. Every time one of the scientists tries to explain some detail about the magnetic field inducer, he'll just wave his hand and say, 'Maybe my son could follow that, but not me.'"

His son? Meaning Michael, and not Peter? He couldn't imagine his dad telling anyone that he was any kind of genius. He looked at Randall doubtfully. *Hypothesis: adults will tell you pretty much anything when they're trying to make you feel better.*

"So maybe when you grow up, you can invent some kind of planetary magnetic field that doesn't crap out on us, eh?" Randall said, separating a few of the multicolored wires. "Hand me the microlaser."

Michael handed him the handheld laser. "I don't want to invent stuff. I want to join the Service."

"Ah," Randall said. "In that case, you're all set. The academy will snap you up in a heartbeat."

"I doubt it," Michael said. He folded his arms and

looked down at the ground. "Environment suit anxiety isn't exactly a quality they look for."

"Suit anxiety? That's what the doctors told you?"

"Yeah," Michael said. He clenched his jaw. "They all say I ought to stay inside the colony."

"Mmm," Randall said. "Obviously you haven't followed *that* advice. And so far it seems to be working out for you."

"Tell my dad that, the next time you see him."

Randall snapped the radio closed and stood up. "Really? He doesn't want you to join the Service?"

"Sure he does," Michael said. "Someday. When I'm better. Which is his way of saying *never.* Because how often does someone with suit anxiety get better enough to go into the Rescue Service?"

"Well, how often does someone with suit anxiety survive for two days out on the surface, in the middle of the biggest natural disaster Mars has ever seen?"

"We were lucky," Michael insisted.

"If you say so."

Randall put the remaining tools back in the toolbox and turned on the radio. The antenna started to swivel around slowly. Every time it pointed in their direction, they could hear a high-pitched ping over the emergency channel in their radios.

"All set," Randall said.

He opened the outer airlock doors, and they stepped inside. Through the small window in the inner doors, Michael could see Lilith waiting for them.

"Hey," he said when the doors opened. "Is everything—"

"A jumpship!" she said. "I found a *jumpship.*"

"It turns out there's some kind of hangar right down this hall," she said breathlessly, leading Michael toward the back of the homestead. "You've got to type in an access code, but someone wrote it on the wall right here."

She entered a code into a panel next to a large set of doors. The panel beeped and the doors slid open. The hangar was dark, but in the light from the hallway they could see a blue tarp covering something that reached almost all the way to the ceiling. The tarp had been pulled partly aside, revealing one of the landing legs and the big engine nozzle of a jumpship.

"I didn't touch it," she said. "It was already like that."

Michael pulled off his helmet and shone his flashlight around the hangar. Tiny particles of dust swirled in the beam from his light. Other than the jumpship, there were a couple of rusted fuel tanks and some shelves that were lined with tools and parts.

"It's in pretty bad shape," Randall said from behind them. "It may not even fly."

"How do you know?" Lilith demanded.

"Because I checked it out before you two arrived."

Lilith's jaw dropped open. "You knew about this? And you didn't tell us?"

"What's there to tell? It's a piece of junk."

"But what if it *does* work?" Michael asked. "Maybe it could take us to Milankovic. Or even all the way back to Heimdall."

"I wouldn't fly in that thing unless my life depended on it," Randall said. "Even if you could get the engine started, you'd have to fly under complete manual control. There are no navigation satellites, remember? So that ship's nav computer isn't going to know the difference between Milankovic and Minnesota. How would I know *where* to fly?"

"Michael could navigate," Lilith said.

"Sure, with a little time he could work out the initial trajectory. But flying by hand, we'd need to make course corrections. That means recalculating the entire arc on the fly—literally."

"He could do it," she insisted. "Right?"

Michael bit his lip. "Maybe."

"Listen, you're a bright kid," Randall said. "But a jumpship is basically a ballistic missile. If we don't get the braking just right, we'll make a crater the size of Omaha. And if we're off by even a few degrees on the course, we could end up farther from Milankovic than we are right now. It's too dangerous."

Lilith shrugged. "All right, whatever. I just thought it was worth looking at."

"Right now we've got food, water, air, and shelter," Randall said. "All we've got to do is stay safe and wait for someone to come get us."

He turned and headed back toward the common room. Lilith folded her arms and leaned against the wall of the hangar. She looked at Michael and raised her eyebrows.

"You want to check it out, don't you?" Michael asked. He sighed and glanced back in the direction Randall had gone. "All right. Get your helmet. But be quiet, okay?"

"Got it," she said, slipping back into the hallway.

Michael found the switch for the overhead lights and pulled off the tarp. The jumpship definitely hadn't been well maintained—there were a few missing sections in the engine cowling, and some kind of oil had leaked from the spot where one of the landing legs attached to the cabin—but it wasn't in terrible shape, either. Jumpships like this were expensive enough that they were sometimes kept in service for twenty years or more. Michael had seen lots of cargo hoppers older than this one landing and taking off outside Heimdall.

Lilith came back wearing her air vest and helmet. Michael closed the inner doors and depressurized the hangar. The outer doors slid open, and the tarp flapped wildly for a moment as a gust of wind swept in. Outside, everything was dark except for the faint gleam of starlight.

With a little effort, they got the cabin door open and the access ladder pulled out. Most of the interior was taken up by a cargo area with hooks and bolts for tying down freight and baggage. There were a couple of jump seats on the back wall for passengers, and a small cockpit up front. The control panel looked like it belonged in some dawn-of-spaceflight adventure movie, but the throttle, control stick, and most of the switches were recognizable enough. Back before his panic attacks had started, he'd flown as copilot with his dad in ships not too different from this one.

Michael flipped on the main power. A long series of boot-up messages flashed past on the screen, followed by the system's main menu. Michael poked around until he found the ship's diagnostics.

"Fusion battery is low on charge, but it will last a few trips at least," he said. "There's juice for the engine. Its biggest complaint is hydraulic fluid—I'm guessing that's what leaked out of the fuselage."

"So it's flyable?" Lilith asked.

Michael switched the screen to navigation mode. It paused for a moment and then flashed several error messages. "Randall is right. The computer isn't going to be any help. We'd be flying fully manual."

He activated the runway casters. The cabin vibrated for a moment as the foot of each landing leg rose up slightly, leaving the ship resting on three ball-shaped rollers. He pushed the control stick forward and the ship shuddered and started to roll toward the hangar doors. Craning his neck to make sure that he didn't clip the side of the hangar, he guided the jumpship out onto a small landing pad.

"Does the engine actually work?"

"Only one way to find out."

He flipped on the preheaters and waited for the ready lights to flash green. Then he made sure the thrust controls were all at zero and jabbed the ignite button with his thumb. For a moment, nothing happened.

"No good?" Lilith said with a disappointed expression. "I was hoping we could at least—"

Underneath their feet, the rocket engine coughed and sputtered. Something clanked once, twice, and then a third time, and then everything was silent except for a faint rumbling in the floor of the cabin.

"We're hot," Michael said, grinning.

A tremendous vibration ran through the ship. Everything that wasn't firmly attached to the walls or floors started to rattle. White smoke drifted up from cracks in the floor of the cabin. Michael and Lilith grabbed onto the pilot's seat.

"What's going on?" Lilith asked.

"I'm not sure," he said, trying to keep his voice level. He checked through the diagnostics on the pilot's control screen. Other than the low hydraulic fluid, the ship wasn't reporting anything wrong. He pressed the button to kill the engine. The vibration stopped, but smoke continued to pour into the cabin.

"Michael . . ."

He waved his hand in front of his helmet to clear the smoke and looked around the cabin. How could anything be burning? The Martian atmosphere was almost entirely CO_2, which was what you used inside colonies to put fires *out.*

"Go," he said, pushing her toward the cabin door.

The interior of the jumpship was now thick with smoke. They stumbled down the ladder onto the landing pad. White clouds billowed all around them, swirling and gusting in the wind. Michael spun around, trying to figure out the source of the smoke, but it seemed to be coming from everywhere.

Something hissed loudly, like a faucet that had just

been turned on. The smoke grew even thicker, and then the hissing stopped and everything was silent. Slowly the smoke cleared, revealing Randall standing next to the fuselage holding a fire extinguisher. An access panel on one side of the ship was open, and everything inside was covered with a thick layer of fire-suppressant foam.

Randall slammed the panel shut. "I guess I assumed that when I said, 'This ship is too dangerous to fly,' that could reasonably be interpreted as 'The two of you shouldn't try to fly it.' But apparently I need to be even more explicit?"

Michael and Lilith looked at each other. "We were just making sure the engine would light," Michael mumbled.

"Well, it lit," Randall said. "Along with a few liters of hydraulic fluid, looks like. So tell me, do the two of you actually *think* about things before you do them?"

"Sorry," Lilith said. "We didn't mean—"

"I've dug enough graves in my life," Randall snapped. "I don't want to dig yours too. Get inside. I'll clean up this mess."

Lilith jogged back toward the airlock. Michael took a few uncertain steps and looked back at Randall, wondering if he should offer to help. But Randall didn't seem interested in the ship. He walked over to an array of solar panels and wiped a thin layer of dust from each panel. When he was done, he looked up at the night sky with a worried expression. Michael followed his gaze, wondering what he was looking at, but all he could see was stars—there was no sign of a ship, or even a satellite.

He squinted. There *were* stars, but only about half as many as he would have expected. The ones that were visible twinkled and pulsed, sometimes almost vanishing before reappearing again.

Michael's stomach lurched. Now he understood why Randall looked worried. There was only one explanation for what he was seeing. "It's a dust storm," he blurted out.

Startled, Randall turned toward him. "I thought I told you to go inside."

"That's what's happening, isn't it?" Michael asked. "The wind off the ice cap is stirring up dust."

Randall pursed his lips. "Looks like it. What I don't understand is why we're getting a storm now. It's completely out of season for this area."

Michael scanned the night sky, trying to estimate how much dust was in the air. Right now it was only blocking out some of the fainter stars. But if the wind stayed like this, and the dust kept getting thicker . . .

Randall put his hand on Michael's shoulder. "Don't

worry too much. We've got our radio beacon going. They'll find us." He sounded as if he was trying to convince himself as much as Michael.

But rescue ships weren't what Michael was worried about. By tomorrow night, the night sky would be completely black with dust. Without any stars to help him, he'd have no way to know which direction Milankovic was in.

Which meant if he was going to climb to the top of the ice cap and get a signal to his father, it would have to be tonight.

12

SNEAKING OUT OF the homestead turned out to be easier than he'd expected. As soon as he was sure Lilith was asleep, he crept out into the hallway and out to the main airlock, making sure to take a route that didn't go past Randall's room. He had an excuse planned if either of them caught him: he'd heard something knocking on the airlock door and wanted to check it out. But it wasn't necessary. Lilith remained fast asleep, and the door to Randall's room stayed closed.

He left a hastily scribbled note for Lilith, explaining what he was doing and telling her not to worry. She'd probably still freak out if she woke up and found it, but at least she'd have some idea where he'd gone. And if everything went well, he'd be back at the homestead in a couple of hours without anyone even knowing that he'd left.

The radio was awkward to carry, and he'd need both his hands free to help him climb, so he brought along an oil-covered tool bag that he'd found in the hangar. He felt a pang of guilt when he dismantled the jury-rigged beacon that Randall had set up. But the beacon would only reach someone who was nearby and already searching for them. *His* plan was going to get a signal all the way to Milankovic. And of course as soon as he got back, he'd set up the beacon again.

The rutted path they'd taken off the ice cap and down to the abandoned homestead was easy enough to follow back up again. The slope grew steeper until the black hulk of the ice cap blotted out almost everything in front of him. The wind got stronger the higher he went, snapping back and forth fitfully. Several times he had to wipe a layer of dust and ice particles off his helmet so he could see clearly.

He stopped when the road began to curve toward the research station. He didn't know whether the magnetic inducer was still putting out enough heat to be dangerous, but he didn't want to find out. The station wasn't high enough up, anyway—he would have to make it all the way to the peak of the glacier if he wanted to get a clear signal to Milankovic. He slung the bag with the radio over his shoulders like a backpack and started to climb directly up the slope.

Back in the homestead, it had seemed like no big deal—just follow the path as far as he could, and then climb the last few hundred meters up to the top. But climbing a few hundred meters in near-total darkness was a lot harder than he'd expected. The light on his helmet was angled to show things in front of him, not above him, and so every few meters he had to pause to crane his neck back and search for the easiest route upward. After ten minutes, he had a stitch in his side, and after twenty minutes, his legs felt like rubber.

It could be worse, he told himself. *At least I'm not climbing under Earth gravity.*

He looked back the way he'd come. The light from the homestead had disappeared in the darkness. Somewhere back there, Lilith and Randall were still sleeping peacefully. He hoped.

The ice cap trembled underneath him, so gently that at first he thought his wrist screen was sounding a quiet alert. The vibration stopped for a few seconds and then started up again.

The hair on the back of Michael's neck stood on end. Was the glacier still melting? Or was the ice just settling? He knelt down and put his hand on the ground and waited, but the vibration didn't return. Cautiously, he stood and looked up at the sky. By tomorrow night the dust storm would turn the sky completely black. If he didn't get a signal to his dad tonight, he'd lose his chance.

He resumed his climb. After thirty more minutes, he crested a small ridge and looked around. He'd reached the peak of the glacier. From this spot, he should have a clear line of sight to Milankovic.

Excitedly, he looked up at the stars and tried to get his bearings. Milankovic was south-southwest from his current position. Michael found the spot in the constellation Cygnus that marked due north and carved out a simple compass rose in the ice with his knife, finally adding a long arrow pointing in the direction of Milankovic. He looked off toward the horizon, hoping he'd be able to catch a glimmer of light from the colony, but all he saw was blackness and swirling dust.

He knelt down and pulled the radio out of the bag. The external antenna was designed to be attached to something solid, like a roof or wall, so he had to use a few chunks of ice to prop it up. Carefully he aimed it along the arrow he'd drawn so that it pointed directly toward the colony. After a few minutes of digging through the options on the radio's screen, he figured out how to link it with his suit radio so that it acted as a signal enhancer.

There was a burst of static, and then a snatch of voices: ". . . south of you . . . Frank would know . . ." Michael sucked in his breath. He was getting a signal!

"Hello, this is Michael Prasad," he said over the emergency channel. "Can anyone hear me?"

There was another puff of static. ". . . hear . . . power . . . negative . . ."

Were they receiving his signal? Michael couldn't tell. Randall had said that if the radio had line of sight, it should reach far enough. Maybe it wasn't pointed in the right direction?

He turned the antenna a fraction of a degree, and suddenly the signal was clearer. "Say again?" a woman's voice said. "Not reading you."

"This is Michael Prasad," he said. "I'm on the ice cap—"

"Prasad?" the woman asked. "Did you say Prasad? Hold on."

A powerful tremble ran through the ice cap. The chunks of ice propping up the radio rattled against each other. Michael grabbed the antenna and tried to hold it steady.

"Yes, Prasad," he repeated. "Michael Prasad. Please, send help. We're stranded near the magnetic field station."

There was no reply. Was she intentionally ignoring him? "Hello? Can you hear me?"

A new voice came over the radio, and Michael's breath caught in his throat. "This is Manish Prasad," his father said.

"Dad?" A dizzying rush of joy and relief and excitement flooded over him. "Dad, it's me! It's Michael!"

"We're not getting a clear signal," his father said. "Who is this? I sure hope this isn't some—"

With a deep rumble, the ice underneath Michael's feet shifted. The antenna turned slightly to one side, and his dad's voice disappeared in a roar of static.

"Dad!" Frantically he tried to reorient the antenna. "Dad, can you hear me?"

More static, and garbled words: ". . . satellites down . . . northeast . . . dust . . ."

"Dad!" he screamed.

The slope he was standing on trembled violently. In the darkness to his right, he heard a loud *crack*. He turned his headlamp just in time to see a massive sinkhole appear in the ice.

For a moment, he was frozen in shock. How could he

have been so stupid? The heat from the magnetic inducer was still melting the glacier from the bottom up, forming air pockets that put stress on the layers above. Now the equilibrium of ice and water and air had begun to shift, and it wouldn't stop until balance had been restored.

The glacier was collapsing.

Michael jammed the radio into the bag and slung it over his shoulder. He leaped off the ridge he was standing on, landing on a flat area a few meters across. Behind him, another large chunk of ice collapsed and fell away. He found a couple of handholds and started to climb down as quickly as he could.

After a few minutes, his fingers were already cramping from the effort of clinging to the slope. This was a steeper route than the path he'd taken while climbing up, and in some places the ice was already cracked and splintered and would fall away at the barest touch. Several times he lost his grip, sliding for a few seconds before he managed to dig his toes into the ice to stop himself.

He'd barely climbed twenty meters downward when he heard a deep rumbling sound from high above. A cloud of tiny ice particles swept past him, followed by larger chunks. A piece of ice struck his shoulder, and he cried out in pain. He clung to the face of the cliff, pressing his body as close to the ice as he could.

A series of snapping and cracking sounds moved

through the ice all around him. For a moment, the air was quiet and still, and then the cliff face began to move. He dug his fingers into the ice, but everything around him was sliding down the slope. He screamed as something ground against his back, digging into him like a knife. He tumbled sideways and began to fall. For a moment he was suspended in a cloud of ice and snow, and then he hit the ground hard.

Michael lay there, half buried in snow, for several seconds. Every breath hurt. He shifted his arm to try to sit up and gasped as icy-cold pain exploded in his shoulder. He reached back with his other hand and felt at the fabric of his suit, already terrified at what he would find.

His suit had a long tear running from his shoulder blades to the small of his back. The material had resealed itself, but every time he moved his arms, part of the tear would split open again, letting in the searingly cold air. He could already taste the metallic tang of the Martian atmosphere where it had mixed with the air of his suit. How long would the filter in his air unit be able to scrub out the deadly carbon dioxide that was seeping in? The leak was large enough that if the filter became saturated, he would die from air poisoning within minutes.

But that wasn't his only problem. The thermal insulation of his suit had been compromised. The skin on his back and shoulders was already numb, and a crackling, icy pain was spreading through his arms and legs. It wouldn't be long before hypothermia set in. If he didn't get back inside the homestead soon, he would freeze to death.

Quickly, he started to climb downward. He didn't have time to be careful; already he could feel his fingers stiffening as the cold spread through his hands. He slid from foothold to foothold, almost skidding down the slope. His fingers missed a handhold, and he fell several meters before scrabbling to a halt. How far had he come? He squinted downward into the darkness, but the base of the ice cap was nowhere in sight.

His body shivered uncontrollably. "Lilith!" he called hoarsely over the emergency band on his suit radio. "Randall! Can you hear me?"

There was no response. They had no idea he was out here, because he'd broken the one cardinal rule of the Martian surface: don't go *anywhere* alone. By the time they realized he wasn't inside the homestead, he'd be nothing more than an ice-covered corpse.

He took a long, deep breath, and then another. A pleasant warmth settled over him. Had the suit managed to repair itself? Maybe his situation wasn't as bad as he'd thought. He could just rest here for a little while and then keep going when he'd regained his strength. All he needed was few minutes, and he'd be ready to go.

He shook his head and snapped awake. The dreamlike warmth disappeared. He swallowed hard as he realized how close he'd come to freezing to death. His suit hadn't repaired itself—that pleasant feeling had just been the beginnings of hypothermia. He stood up and flexed his arms and legs, trying to get the blood to circulate. He had to keep moving, no matter what. If he stopped again, he would die.

He started to half run, half jump down the slope, using his headlamp to pick out any spot that seemed flat enough to stand on. Carbon dioxide snow, scattered in a thin layer on top of the rock and ice, flashed into vapor from the warmth of his boots. He ran faster, hardly paying attention to where he landed. Faster. He had to move faster.

Suddenly he was on a wide, flat trail. He'd reached the base of the slope. He took a few steps and fell to his knees, breathing hard. Every muscle and fiber in his body wanted desperately to lie down and sleep. He crawled forward along the path, barely managing to put one hand in front of the other.

That way. Keep going that way.

But the homestead was almost a kilometer away. He wasn't going to make it. His body was shutting down. At any moment he would collapse and never get up again.

"Michael!" a voice shouted.

Lights appeared in front of him. Two suited figured ran up the path. One of them was Lilith, he realized. The other one he couldn't recognize. "Dad?" he croaked.

"It's me," Randall said, crouching down next to him. Hands probed his back and arms and the two voices talked quickly back and forth.

"In shock," Michael muttered. "Hy-po-therm-ia."

"Michael, you have to walk," Lilith said. "Do you hear me? You have to stand up and walk."

"Walk," Michael agreed, but he didn't move. Moving was too difficult.

Randall and Lilith dragged him to his feet. He moaned in protest and stumbled along with them toward the homestead. His head lolled to one side and rested on Lilith's shoulder.

"Keep going," she said. "Just keep going."

Bright lights. The hiss of an airlock. Warm air flooding over his skin as someone pulled off his helmet. They sat him down in a chair, and Randall pressed an injector against his arm. After a few seconds, the numb, cadaverous feeling in his body started to fade, as if he had crossed some invisible line between half dead and half alive.

A cup of hot liquid was pressed against Michael's lips. He drank and gasped in pain as the heat made its way down his throat. They applied a patch to his suit and then wrapped him in blankets with his arms tight across his chest, taking turns forcing him to drink something—hot chocolate, he finally realized—until he sputtered and turned his head away.

"How do you feel?" Randall asked, watching him intently.

Hot. Cold. Numb. In agony. Nothing Michael could say would describe the conflicting sensations coming from his body right now, so he just shook his head.

"Where did you go?" Lilith asked. "What were you thinking?"

"Radio," Michael mumbled. "Wanted t' get a signal."

"In the middle of the night?" Lilith fumed. Randall put his hand on her shoulder, but she shook him away. "You've done a lot of dumb things in your short life, but this has to be the most boneheaded, thick-skulled, immensely stupid thing I've ever heard of."

"You're lucky Lilith woke up," Randall said. "She was ready to run out there alone—I barely managed to persuade her to put on a helmet."

Lilith muttered something unintelligible in response, though Michael was pretty sure he caught the words "idiotic" and "reckless" and a few choice bits of profanity.

"Did you reach anyone?" Randall asked. "Do they know we're here?"

Michael tried to remember. "I'm not sure. There was a lot of interference."

"Where is the radio now?"

"I can answer that one," Lilith said. "The radio is right here."

She emptied out the bag Michael had been carrying. Inside was a collection of circuit boards, wires, and processing chips. It looked less like a radio and more like a collection of parts from an electronics store.

"Or at least what *used* to be the radio."

13

"SO LET ME make sure I've got this straight." Lilith kicked a chair, sending it spinning into a corner of the kitchen. "Not only did you go outside on your own and nearly get yourself killed, but you also managed to destroy our *only way of contacting anyone.*"

She was right. His trip up to the top of the ice cap had cost them their only long-distance radio. And what had he gotten out of it? A ten-second conversation with his dad. Not even a *conversation,* really, since as far as he could tell, it had been completely one-sided. His dad hadn't even known who he was talking to.

At least now he knew his father was safe. That was something. But right now wasn't the time to argue over the details. "I'm sorry," he said quietly.

"Oh, you're sorry?" Lilith said, throwing up her hands. "I didn't realize that. I don't suppose *sorry* is going to fix this radio?"

"Leave him be," Randall said. "There's nothing we can do about it now."

Randall reached out and checked Michael's pulse. He nodded and glanced at Lilith. "The patch is clean and the injection I gave him seems to be working, but one of us needs to stay awake to keep an eye on him. Do you want the first shift, or the second?"

"I'm not sleeping anytime soon," Lilith said. "I'll take the first shift."

Michael didn't think he was going to be able to sleep either, but he wasn't going to argue with getting some rest. He lay down on the floor of their room and stared up at the ceiling. Lilith sat in the corner, watching him with her arms folded.

"I shouldn't have gone up there by myself," he said.

"Nope," Lilith replied. "So what you need to do now is apply that brain of yours to getting us home safely."

He nodded, though he had no idea how he was going to manage *that*. The three of them were stuck here until someone found them. After what had happened at the station, they were lucky to be alive. And now, on top of everything else, they had a freak dust storm to worry about.

Randall was right—it was unusual to have a storm like this so late in the year. Was there some explanation, or was it just a random occurrence? The weather on Mars was usually simple and easy to forecast, thanks to the dry, thin air. It was nothing like Earth, where the massive oceans and constant evaporation made the weather almost impossible to predict far in advance.

He was just drifting off to sleep when a thought went through his head. *Evaporation.*

What would happen on Mars if a million tons of water vapor were suddenly added to the atmosphere?

"Michael," Lilith said, rocking him gently by the shoulder. "Michael, wake up."

Michael opened his eyes and looked around. Everything was pitch-black except for a faint glow from down the hallway. He reached out and felt Lilith kneeling next to him.

"What's going on?" he asked blearily.

"The lights went out about a half hour ago," she said. "Randall said the power system wasn't working well, so I wasn't too worried at first. But now the air seems to be going bad."

Michael took a deep breath. She was right—the air

tasted stale and tinny. Was he already a little lightheaded, or was that just an aftereffect of the hypothermia? He fumbled around until he found his helmet and snapped it into place. He took a few deep breaths to clear his lungs. *You're okay,* he told himself. *Just stay relaxed.* Hopefully Randall could figure out what was wrong with the air in the homestead and they'd be able to take off their helmets again.

"Randall?" Lilith said, standing in the doorway of the room across the hall. "Are you awake? The power's gone completely out."

Randall lifted his head and blinked in the glare of her headlamp. He stared at her for a moment, and then looked around. "Dammit," he said. *"Dammit."*

"Sorry to wake you up," Lilith said. "But the air—"

"You did the right thing." Randall stood up and rubbed his jaw. "I'm an idiot for not making sure the air-quality alarms were still working. If it wasn't for you, we might have never woken up."

He put on his own helmet, and they followed him into an equipment room next to the hangar. A large barrel-shaped battery sat next to racks of ancient-looking computer hardware. Everything was covered in dust except for a small workstation perched on a plastic cart. Randall pulled a chair over to the workstation and turned the screen on. He scanned over a few pages' worth of diagnostic data, and then he let out a long sigh.

"It's the dust storm," he said. "The solar panels aren't getting enough sunlight, and these batteries are barely holding a charge."

"Is that bad?" Lilith asked.

"It's not good," Randall said. "It means we'll have to sleep with our helmets on."

Lilith looked at Michael with concern. "You going to be okay with that?"

"Wearing a helmet all night long, in a pitch-black, underground room the size of a large closet?" he said with a weak smile. "Sure? Who wouldn't be?"

But panic attacks weren't the only thing on his mind. The more they used their suits' air units, the more saturated their CO_2 filters would get. Their air vests had less than an hour of reserve oxygen left. When the scrubbers finally gave out . . .

"We'll be okay as long as this dust storm doesn't get any worse," Randall said. But he had a worried look in his eye that told Michael he was thinking about their air filters too.

Michael suddenly remembered what had been going through his head right before he fell asleep. "I don't think we can count on that. I think I know what's causing this storm."

"You do?" Randall asked, cocking his head.

"The heat from the magnetic inducer was melting that glacier, right? I'll bet it was enough to cause a lot of the water to evaporate into the atmosphere."

"Like how storms form on Earth?" Lilith said.

"Exactly," Michael said. "Check the humidity and pressure outside. I'll bet they're both off the charts."

Randall tapped at the screen. "You're right," he said, frowning. "I've never seen readings like this."

"Hurricanes get their energy from the sun heating the water," Lilith said. "I studied this back in third grade. Once they move over land, there's no more evaporation to power them, and they die out. But if this one is getting its heat from the magnetic inducer, and the inducer is getting its energy from the flare . . ."

"The storm won't stop until the flare dies out," Randall finished in a quiet voice. Now even his pretense that everything was going to be okay had disappeared.

"How long is that going to be?" Michael asked.

"I don't know," Randall said. "We've never had a flare like this. From the way it's still going, I'd guess a few more days at least. Maybe longer."

"Oh," Lilith said, looking a little pale.

"For the moment, we're safe in here," Randall said. "As long as the batteries can charge up enough to last most of the night, we'll be okay."

"But what if the storm gets worse?" Lilith said.

"If the storm gets worse, we'll figure out something else. Till then, we just sit tight."

Michael lay back down on the floor of their bedroom, but between his anxiety about the helmet and his worry about their situation overall, it was impossible for him to sleep. Out of boredom he started to go over some of the calculations for a jumpship trajectory. He checked the map on his wrist screen. Milankovic was three hundred thirty kilometers away, south-southwest. If the jumpship had a thrust-to-weight ratio of six to one . . .

He was double-checking his calculations when Lilith sat up abruptly and pulled at her collar. "I'm starting to understand why you hate these things so much."

"You can't sleep either?"

"No," she said. "Though it doesn't help that you keep muttering random numbers to yourself."

"Oh," he said. "Sorry."

"Any idea how long it will be till the power comes on?"

"The sun came up thirty minutes ago. So it should be . . ." He paused briefly as the lights flickered on. "Right about now, actually."

"Michael Prasad, you truly are a genius," she said, rolling her eyes.

It took another fifteen minutes before the filters in the homestead had scrubbed the air enough for it to be breathable. Michael and Lilith heated up three pouches of vegetable curry while Randall checked over the electrical systems. Finally he declared that the air was "good enough" and they took off their helmets and ate ravenously.

"Do you think the power will stay on until tonight?" Lilith asked.

"It'll last till the sun goes down," Randall said. "But not much longer than that."

Lilith groaned. "So we're sleeping in our helmets again?"

"That's one option," Randall said slowly. He turned toward Michael. "The other is that we fix up that jump-ship and fly it to Milankovic."

"Fly it?" Michael repeated. "You mean, tonight?"

Randall nodded. "As soon as the sun goes down—if you're still sure that you can handle the navigation."

Michael had a sudden nervous feeling in the pit of his stomach. It had been one thing to think about a ballistic course as a theoretical exercise. The math wasn't that complicated—nineteenth-century artillery crews had done it long before computers had been invented.

But even if the principle was the same, there was a big difference between firing off a mortar shell and hand-piloting a jumpship. Especially one that the three of them would be flying on.

"Two days ago you were all fired up about how dangerous that jumpship is," Lilith said. "Now you're in a hurry to fly it out of here?"

Randall was silent for a moment. "The situation has changed. If Michael can handle the navigation, then I think it's our best bet."

"He can handle it," Lilith said, sounding much more confident than Michael felt at the moment. "Right?"

The two of them looked at him expectantly. Michael took a deep breath and tried to ignore the anxiety that was building up deep inside him.

"Of course," he said. "No problem."

It felt strange to think that soon they'd be leaving this place behind. They'd been here only a few days, and for most of that time he'd been cold, hungry, and uncomfortable, but Michael had grown oddly attached to the little homestead. He did his best to clean up while Lilith collected supplies.

"Fourteen packets of expired energy gel and twenty-two pouches of expired water," Lilith said, coming out of a storeroom with a large box. "Plus two expired medical kits in case we break a leg or something."

"I wonder if we should leave a note," Michael said. "Even though it'd probably be twenty years before anyone read it."

"That's taken care of," Lilith said, tearing a few sheets out of a notebook. "I've been keeping a log ever since we got here."

"You have?"

Lilith shrugged. "Nothing else to do but read textbooks and fifty-year-old romance novels. Anyway, I wanted to leave some kind of record of what happened to us."

"If we don't make it back, you mean," Michael said.

"Yeah. Except that's not going to happen, because that crazy-smart brain of yours is going to get us to Milankovic, where I am going to eat everything in the world other than vegetable curry and energy gel."

"The ship is prepped," Randall said, poking his head into the kitchen. "Are you ready?"

"As we'll ever be," Lilith said.

As he followed Randall and Lilith back toward the hangar, Michael's stomach started to churn. Was this really the right thing to do? Maybe if they just set up a new beacon and stayed in the homestead, someone would be here soon to rescue them.

You'll be fine, he thought grimly. *Maybe you can't do anything else, but you can do math, right?*

The sun had just set, and the sky was a deep reddish-brown that was quickly fading to black. Randall had already moved the ship out onto the little landing pad outside the hangar. The preheat cycle of the engines had melted a wide, slushy circle in the ice that had collected on the pad. They waded out to the boarding ladder and climbed inside. Michael sat in the copilot's station, and Lilith unfolded one of the jump seats on the rear cabin wall. Randall pulled three hypo-injector tubes out of his pocket and stuffed them into the bag with the medical supplies.

"What are those for?" Lilith asked.

He shoved the kit into a small recess on the rear cabin wall. "Radiation poisoning is not a pleasant way to go. If we get stuck out there, I want a backup option."

Michael cocked his head and frowned. "So those will help? What's in them?"

"Two hundred milligrams of pseudomorphine for each of us," Randall said. "Enough to make it quick and painless."

"Oh," Lilith said. She and Michael exchanged a look. Radiation poisoning wasn't a pleasant thought. But the idea of needing a "backup option" wasn't pleasant, either.

Michael unfolded the scrap of paper where he'd

written his final course. He'd gone over his calculations a half dozen times. Everything was correct, mathematically speaking. But real life wasn't the same as mathematics. Even if Randall got the thrust exactly right, they weren't going to be flying on a perfect parabolic curve. The engines were old. The attitude rockets might not be able to get the nose of the ship pointing in the exact direction they needed. And there was the wind to take into account, and . . .

"Time for that trajectory," Randall said as he strapped himself into the pilot's seat.

Michael nodded and handed the slip of paper to him. Randall looked it over and glanced back at Lilith. She gave a thumbs-up. "All good back here."

Randall flipped on the power. The pilot's and copilot's screens flashed through a boot-up sequence, and then they displayed an error message. *No navigation satellites available.* The message was bright and bold and red, as if to make it perfectly clear how stupid it was to fly a jumpship without a working nav computer. Michael wondered what the ship's original programmers would say if they knew someone was going to fly a course that had been hand calculated by a twelve-year-old kid.

A sharp tremor ran through the ship, and Michael

jerked upright in his seat. He settled back down again awkwardly as he realized that it was just Randall starting the main engine.

"You okay?" Randall asked.

"I'm fine."

Except that he wasn't. A cold drop of sweat ran down the back of his neck. He tried to take deep, slow breaths, but an all-too-familiar feeling of inescapable terror was building up at the back of his mind.

No. Not now. This couldn't happen to him now.

He'd almost forgotten what a panic attack was like. His chest felt as if someone were squeezing him in a vise. He leaned forward and grabbed the copilot's controls to steady himself.

I can't I can't I can't

"Michael?"

The voice was so distant that he wasn't sure whether it was Randall or Lilith. Darkness crept in around the corners of his vision until he could hardly see anything other than the control panel in front of him. The only sound he could hear was the pounding of his own heartbeat. Suddenly there was nothing in the world more important than getting off the ship. He unbuckled his harness and ran toward the hatchway.

Behind him, he heard Randall and Lilith shouting. He jumped down onto the landing pad and sprinted for the airlock at the back of the hangar. As soon as he was inside, he jerked open the collar of his helmet and tore it off his head. He sat down with his back against the wall and sucked in deep lungfuls of air.

The light on the airlock flashed and the door slid open. Lilith ran to him and knelt down. "What happened? Are you all right?"

"I'm sorry," he whispered, clenching his eyes shut so that he wouldn't have to see the disappointment on her face. "I'm so sorry, Lil. I can't do it."

14

MICHAEL WOKE THE next morning feeling as if he'd slept for a hundred years and could sleep for a hundred more. He sat up and looked around blearily. The room was dark, but a light down the hallway meant that the sun had risen and the solar panels were providing power. He checked the air quality on his wrist display and found that the oxygen levels were even lower than they'd been the previous morning. He rolled his neck and shoulders to work out the kinks. How long would it be before he could sleep without a helmet?

He wished he could give Lilith and Randall some kind of reason for why he'd panicked yesterday. But he couldn't even explain *why* being on that jumpship had been so frightening. He'd felt exactly the same way as when he'd had his very first panic attack, back when he was ten. Except that instead of his brain deciding that putting on an environment suit would kill him, this time it had freaked out over sitting in the cockpit of a jumpship. It didn't make sense.

He opened the door and headed down to the kitchen. Lilith was sitting at the table with her feet propped up, reading on her screen. She glanced up at him and gave a little nod.

"Breakfast will be ready in a bit. Anything you want as long as it's vegetable curry."

He filled up a water pouch at the sink and drank it through the port in his helmet. It tasted warm and metallic, but he didn't really care. He sat down and laid his head on the table. Maybe he did need more sleep.

"You know, I've been reading up on environment suit anxiety," Lilith said.

Michael looked up at her and frowned. "You have?"

"Yep. And I've come to the conclusion that you don't actually have it."

"You think that I don't have suit anxiety?"

"Exactly."

"Lilith—"

"Don't get me wrong, you've clearly got *some* kind of

panic disorder," she said, holding up her hands. "But look at it this way—what's the defining characteristic of suit anxiety?"

"Anxiety while wearing a suit?"

"Anxiety while wearing a suit!" she exclaimed, banging her fist on the table. "Exhibit A: Michael Prasad, who has now spent approximately umpty-two hours in a suit, and—if it please the court—is wearing one at *this precise minute,* without any ill effects whatsoever."

Michael had to admit that she had a point. Until yesterday, he hadn't had a panic attack since he'd gone searching for her back in the cave. "Okay, Dr. Colson. If it isn't being in an environment suit that makes me panic, what is it?"

"Well, that's the question, isn't it? So let's start at the beginning. Tell me about your very first panic attack. You said it happened when you tried to take the suit test?"

"Yeah," Michael said. "I'd been out onto the surface fifty or sixty times already by then. It was going to be a piece of cake."

"When did it start? Out on the surface, or when you were in the prep room putting on your suit?"

He thought for a moment. "Well, neither, actually. I think it really started the night before the test. I felt this kind of dread, like I *knew* something was going to go wrong."

"The night before," she mused. "That's interesting. Not quite what you'd expect, is it? That you would start feeling suit anxiety twelve hours before you put on a suit?"

"I suppose."

"After that, your dad kept trying to take you outside?"

"Yeah," he said. "Five or six times. But I never even made it out of the airlock."

"Let's jump forward to a few days ago, when you took the test again. You were fine out on the surface, right? Up until the end?"

"I was a little anxious," he said. "But it wasn't too bad until the navigation section."

"Do you remember what you were feeling right before you started to panic?"

He shrugged. "I guess I was nervous I was going to fail the test."

"Mmm," she said. "And what about the other night on the rover?"

"I had a dream," he said, thinking back. "A nightmare, I guess. About my dad taking me outside, over and over."

"Then you woke up, and *blammo*." She nodded. "I think

we're getting somewhere. Now, tell me about yesterday."

"Well, yesterday was different," he said. "I was doing fine until we got onto the jumpship. I gave Randall my calculations, and suddenly . . ."

"Blammo?"

"Yeah," he said. "Blammo. So, Dr. Colson, what's your diagnosis?"

She leaned back in her seat and pressed the tips of her fingers together. "Well, I don't think it's the suit that makes you panic," she said. "I think it's the pressure."

He looked at her confusedly. "I always set the air pressure to—"

"No," she said, rolling her eyes. "I mean the *pressure*. On you. Like when you took the test the first time, it was supposed to be a walk in the park, right? You're Michael Prasad, Boy Genius of Mars. You weren't *allowed* to fail."

"I failed because I couldn't fail?" Michael said doubtfully.

"It does sound kind of crazy, doesn't it?" Lilith said. "But it fits. How did you feel afterward?"

Michael tried to remember. "Like it was the end of the world. Like I'd let everyone down." Most of all, like he'd let his *dad* down.

"And how did you feel yesterday, after your panic attack on the jumpship?" she asked. "Was it the same?"

"Except even worse, because if I screwed up . . ." He

trailed off. This time, if he screwed up, people would die.

"I wish I knew what to say to make you stop feeling that pressure. All I can really tell you is that it's okay to fail," Lilith said. "It's okay to not have all the answers. People aren't going to see you any differently. You're still *you.*"

He nodded. What she was saying made sense, but it still didn't *feel* okay.

Lilith stood up and headed toward the storeroom. When she reached the doorway, she stopped and turned back toward him.

"I guess what I mean is that if I had to pick anyone in the world to navigate that ship, it would be you. But if I had to pick anyone in the world to *not* navigate that ship, it would still be you."

Michael turned this over in his head, trying to figure out what she meant. Why would she want to be here with him, instead of with someone who could actually get them home? *Hypothesis looking likely: sometimes girls say things just to confuse you.*

Michael's stomach rebelled against the idea of another bowl of vegetable curry, so he drank some energy gel and wandered through the hallways at the back of the homestead until he found Randall hunched over a circuit board in a makeshift workshop. Electronic parts, wires, tubes, and plastic containers were scattered over a large table. A small lantern cast long shadows across the room. Randall's helmet was sitting on the table next to him.

"Is the air good to breathe already?" Michael asked.

Randall straightened up quickly and glanced back at him. "It's not too bad. Might give you a little headache. Probably best to wait a little longer."

Michael frowned. If the air quality was still bad enough to give you a headache, why wasn't Randall still wearing his helmet too? "What are you working on?"

"Nothing, really. Just fiddling."

Michael picked up a flat metal cylinder and inspected it. It was obviously old, but looked to be in good shape. "This is an industrial air filter, isn't it?"

"Mmm-hmm." Randall bent back down over the table and stared at the wires coming out of the circuit board.

"How many of these do we have?"

"About forty," Randall said.

Michael understood Randall's frustrated expression. Forty air filters that could make all the air in the entire homestead breathable, but not enough sunlight to power them. Three suits with their own internal power sources, but not enough portable filters to run them. Michael noticed a small fusion battery on the floor, the sort that would power a tram car or a piece of heavy machinery. "You're trying to rig one of them up," he said. "Is it working?"

"Not yet."

"Do you need any help?"

"How well do you understand metal-organic CO_2 absorption systems?"

"Not very well," Michael admitted.

"Me neither," Randall said. "Meaning the chances I'm going to get this to work are somewhere south of five percent. But it's better than staring at the wall."

Suddenly Michael realized what was odd about Randall's suit—his air vest was lying flat and empty against his chest, which meant not only had he used up his reserves, but his suit filter wasn't working well enough to refill the vest with liquid oxygen. Michael leaned over Randall's shoulder until he caught a glimpse of his wrist screen. His skin went cold. *Filter 94% saturated,* it read. *Estimated 22 hours remaining.*

"Do you mind?" Randall said, turning his arm so that his wrist display was hidden. "I'm trying to work here."

"Sorry," Michael mumbled. He paused for a moment. "So everything is okay with your suit?"

"Don't worry about me," Randall said without turning around. "I'm fine."

"You're sure?" Michael asked.

"I may not know much about industrial-strength filters," Randall snapped, "but I know how to read my suit diagnostics. Now would you please give me a little space?"

Michael backed away, trying not to give any indication that he'd noticed the warning message. Why didn't Randall want them to know that his filter was starting to go bad? Was he going to just let himself run out of air?

He stared at Randall, still hunched over the worktable. They couldn't let that happen. Somehow, they were going to find a way to leave—tonight.

15

ROLLED BACK INSIDE the hangar, the jumpship somehow looked larger than it had out on the landing pad. The hatchway above the boarding ladder was still hanging open. Outside the hangar, the setting sun had turned the sky into a wash of red and purple and blue.

Michael climbed inside and sat at the copilot's console. His eyes landed on the piece of paper where he'd written out the trajectory for Randall. His stomach lurched, and he had to fight the urge to tear it into a thousand pieces.

What if Lilith was right? Dr. Chapman had focused on panic attacks from environment suits because up until this trip that had always seemed like the cause. But she had stressed that there could be other factors, and that there was often more to panic disorders than it first appeared.

The more he thought about the panic attack he'd had

the day before, the more he realized that the thought of flying to Milankovic in a rusty jumpship wasn't what terrified him. It was the idea of Randall and Lilith relying on *his* hand-calculated trajectory that made him want to curl up in a ball and close his eyes. It was too much. They were asking too much.

He paused for a moment, letting his hands rest on the controls. An idea formed in the back of his head. Maybe there was a way he could help Randall and Lilith without risking their lives. His heart started to beat more quickly. He reached out and flipped on the main control panel. Everything he needed was right here. . . .

"You just trying everything out?" Lilith said from behind him.

"Oh—hey," Michael said, spinning around in his seat. "Just . . . experimenting."

Lilith cocked her head to one side. She glanced at the control panel and back at him, and then she banged her fist against the hatchway. "No, no, *no*. Please tell me you weren't just about to do the incredibly, ridiculously, impossibly stupid thing I'm pretty sure you were just about to do."

"I wasn't," Michael insisted. But her angry glare seemed to cut right through him, and after a moment he turned back toward the console and sagged against the seat. "All right. I was *thinking* about it."

"Do you remember what happened the last time you decided to go off on your own?" she demanded. "Torn suit, hypothermia, broken radio? Does any of that ring a bell?"

"You sound like my mom," he muttered under his breath.

"I'm serious! I don't understand how you could be so idiotic. Do you just have some kind of compulsion to be a hero?"

"I'm not trying to be a hero!"

"Then why are you in here, getting ready to fly to Milankovic by yourself, when yesterday you had a panic attack before we'd even left the landing pad?"

"Because if I don't, Randall is going to die," Michael said. "I saw his suit diagnostics. His air filter is almost saturated."

Lilith paused. "How long does he have left?"

"Less than a day."

"Oh, god," she said, leaning her helmet back against the wall of the cabin. "All right—we need to do something. But that still doesn't explain why you think the right thing to do is to fly *alone*."

"All I need to do is go get help. I can be back here in a few hours."

"And what if you can't? What if this ship blows up when you're halfway there?"

Michael set his jaw. "Then at least I won't have killed you, too."

"That's not how it works! I'm not some fragile doll you get to leave behind when you think it's too dangerous. If you're going, I'm going."

"I can't do it. Not with you and Randall on the ship. Didn't you see me yesterday? I was *useless*."

He was panicking right now, just thinking about it. The taste of bile seeped into his mouth, and he swallowed hard.

"Hey," she said, her voice suddenly gentle. "Don't be so hard on yourself."

He locked his eyes with Lilith's. There was nothing she could do except be there with him, but somehow that was enough. She was calm and steady, like a rock at the center of a whirlpool. He matched his breathing to hers, taking long, deep breaths in through his nose and out through his mouth. His heart rate slowed and the knot in his stomach unclenched. He could feel the panic hovering around him, just out of sight, but for the moment its hold on him was broken.

"This isn't just like failing a suit test and disappointing your dad, is it?" Lilith said.

"No," he said hoarsely. "I could get us all killed."

Lilith shrugged. "So what? It would be better than dying here, in the dark."

"If I make even a tiny mistake—"

"So what?" she said. "We'll fix it, somehow. You may be ridiculously smart, but you're still human. You can't blame yourself for not being perfect. Especially not before it even happens."

He nodded, but the voice in the back of his head wasn't convinced. It *would* be his fault. He would screw it up, people would die. . . .

Randall climbed up the boarding ladder and stuck his head into the cabin. "What's going on here?"

"Michael was getting ready to fly to Milankovic by himself," Lilith said. Michael glared at her and she shrugged. "He needs to know."

"By *himself?*" Randall asked.

"He seems to think that's easier, somehow."

"Not going to happen," Randall said, shaking his head. "I'll lock him up in his room if I have to."

"Not a bad idea," Lilith said. "But he'd probably just escape. I think we need to come up with something better."

"Hey, I'm right here," Michael said.

Randall cocked his head at Lilith. "Why do I get the feeling that you have a plan of your own?"

"As a matter of fact, I do," she said. "My plan is that all three of us fly out of here, right now."

"We tried that," Randall said. "It didn't go so well."

"Well, we're going to try again, for two reasons," Lilith

said. "First, because I think Michael has gotten it at least partway through his thick skull that he doesn't need to carry the whole world on his shoulders. And second, because we know that if we don't leave tonight, your air filter is going to die sometime tomorrow."

Randall's jaw set. "That's my business. You don't need to worry about it."

"Of course we need to worry about it!" Lilith shouted. "You're being as stupid as he is! In what universe is it okay to risk your own life without even *talking* to the people you're trying to save?"

"She's right," Michael said quietly. "From now on we do whatever it takes to get us all home safely."

Randall was silent for a long moment. "I'm supposed to be the leader here. But it looks like I've been outleadered."

"It happens," Lilith said. "So—what's our plan? How soon do we leave?"

"The sooner, the better," Randall said. "I want us to have as much time as possible before the sun rises."

They restowed all of the supplies and sealed the hatchway and climbed into their seats. Randall picked up the piece of paper where Michael had written their course. He looked over at Michael. "Last chance. You're sure about this?"

Michael looked back at Lilith, and then he nodded. "I'm sure."

Randall flipped a switch and the engines underneath the cabin floor rumbled. White clouds of water vapor billowed out all around the ship. "Takeoff in three . . . two . . . one . . ."

The engine roared. For a moment, nothing else seemed to happen. Then the ship leaped into the air and Michael was jammed down into his seat by the force of the acceleration. He wrapped his arms across his chest and watched the gauges on the copilot's display.

For the hundredth time, his mind reviewed the trajectory he had given to Randall. He knew it was stupid and pointless—if he'd made a mistake, it was too late to fix now—but he couldn't help it. He breathed in and out, slowly and deeply, and tried to tell himself that everything was going to be okay.

"Sixty meters per second," Randall called out. The ship rotated and tilted backward, revealing the vast northern plains, rendered sparkling white by a layer of snow.

"Course is good," Randall said. "Speed one sixty. Forty-four seconds of burn left."

"Smoke!" Lilith shouted.

Michael glanced back. A gray-black haze was filling the cabin. "Nothing we can do about it now," Randall said. "We have to keep accelerating. Call it!"

Michael had been so focused on the trajectory that

he'd completely forgotten about the possibility of a mechanical failure. Was something on fire? Or was this just more ancient hydraulic fluid burning off?

"Call it!" Randall shouted.

Michael turned back to the controls and watched the burn timer. "Five. Four. Three. Two. One. Now!"

Randall pulled back on the throttle, and the engines went silent. Michael's stomach lurched with weightlessness, and he floated up against his safety harness.

"Speed six twelve, altitude nineteen thousand," Randall said. He looked over at Michael. "Will that work?"

Michael thought for a moment, picturing the arc that the ship was now following. "That should put us less than a kilometer away from the colony."

Lilith crowed and clapped her hands. "Nice job, Big M."

Outside the jumpship, the sky was a deep purplish black, with the full array of stars shining down. At this altitude, the horizon was visibly curved, and there were several clusters of yellow-white lights gleaming brightly against the dark surface of the planet. Michael kept his eyes on a small patch of light ahead of them that grew larger and larger with each passing second. *Milankovic*, he thought.

"We'll be heading back down in a minute," Randall said. "What are the deceleration numbers?"

"Thrust at fifteen meters per second squared, starting

at twelve klicks," Michael said. "Total burn forty-five seconds."

Randall nodded. The jumpship reached the peak of its trajectory and started to head back down. Michael gripped the arms of his seat. They'd been weightless ever since the acceleration stopped, but somehow it always felt different when you knew you were plummeting back down toward the ground. He leaned forward and watched the lights of Milankovic until they disappeared beneath the ship.

Was his dad even still there? Did he have any idea that Michael was trying to get to him?

"All right, let's swing back for deceleration," Randall said, typing commands into his screen. "Counter-burns in three, two, one . . ."

He pressed the execute button on his screen. The attitude rockets on the side of the ship coughed and sputtered. The ship gave a brief shudder and kept falling along its trajectory.

"More smoke back here," Lilith called. "Is everything okay?"

"The attitude rockets aren't firing," Randall said. His face was taut. "Michael, take the controls."

"Wait, what?" Michael said.

But Randall was already unbuckling his harness. "Once I give you the word, tilt us back. Lilith, get up here in the pilot's seat."

Michael's hands went clammy. He looked at the altimeter. They were already at thirteen thousand meters. The later they started the burn, the more thrust they would have to use to make up for it. And if they started too late . . .

Randall floated out of the cockpit and back into the main cabin. He helped Lilith strap herself into the pilot's seat and then opened up a hatch in the floor and dug through a tangle of wires and hydraulic lines. Black smoke poured out of the hatch, and he cursed loudly.

The panic that Michael been keeping at bay pushed at the back of his mind like pressure rising in a boiler. They were off course now, which meant Randall would need him to recalculate a new set of burns. He tried to work out a basic set of course adjustments, but his mind refused to cooperate. What had made him think that he was smart enough to navigate a ship like this? He'd been stupid to try. His heart fluttered and he dug his fingers into the sides of his seat.

"It isn't Rosalind Carver!" Lilith shouted from the pilot's console.

Michael stared at her uncomprehendingly. "What?"

"The girl who thinks you're so remarkable. It isn't Rosalind. I just wanted you to know that."

His mouth dropped open. Suddenly his mind was spinning for reasons that had nothing to do with panic or jumpships or danger. Was she bringing this up now just to distract him again? Or was she—

Randall slammed a panel shut at the back of the cabin. "Light the engine!" he shouted. "Push it to one-quarter power."

Michael sat up straight and focused on the copilot's controls. "We're still tilted the wrong way!" he called back. Without the attitude thrusters, the engine was still pointing back the way they'd come. Turning it on would slow their descent, but it would also push them past Milankovic and out into the desert beyond.

"I need time!" Randall yelled, pulling open a second control panel.

Michael started the ignition sequence and slid the throttle forward. The engine roared. The acceleration pushed him back down into his seat. The altimeter, which was now at ten thousand meters, started to drop more slowly. But every second that passed would put them farther from Milankovic when they landed.

If they landed.

Randall pulled a hose free of a coupling, and a blast of steam filled the cabin. "Activate the landing legs!" Michael flipped a switch to deploy the three landing legs, but nothing happened. He peered out the cockpit window. The only leg he could see was still in its retracted spot.

"It didn't work!"

"Check the actuators. Do they have hydraulic pressure?"

Michael glanced at the altimeter—five thousand meters—and then at the pilot's display screen. "Everything is green," he said.

"Then go!" Randall shouted.

Michael hit the execute button. The attitude rockets swiveled and fired. The ship leaned back until the cockpit was facing up toward the stars again and the engine was pointing in the direction they were falling. Randall slid into the jump seat at the rear of the cabin and fastened his harness.

"Full power in three, two, one!" Michael yelled, and then jammed the throttle all the way forward. The sound of the engine rose to a deafening roar, and the ship shuddered violently. Michael was pressed down in his seat so hard that he had to fight to breathe.

Two thousand meters. One thousand. Michael kept his eyes fixed on the altimeter as if he could slow it down by sheer force of will. Five hundred meters. They were still falling way too fast. Two hundred. One hundred.

"Hold on!" he screamed.

16

AM I DEAD?

Michael opened his eyes without remembering when he had closed them. The only light came from the faint glow of stars through the cockpit window. Everything in front of him was a blurry jumble of metal and plastic. His ribs hurt when he breathed, and his right knee throbbed painfully. He turned on his headlamp and blinked several times, trying to get his eyes to clear.

Lilith was slumped down in the pilot's seat with her head lolled to one side. Blood was running down along her chin and smeared on the inside of her helmet, but he couldn't see where it was coming from. Was she breathing? Was she alive?

"Lilith," he mumbled. His tongue was thick, and he

tasted blood. Lilith didn't respond.

He unfastened his harness and climbed across to her seat. Her scalp had been split open just above her ear. The cut disappeared into her hair, which was matted with blood. She was completely motionless, and even with his hand on her chest he couldn't tell whether she was breathing.

Dead she can't be dead she can't be dead

He grabbed her wrist and looked at her screen. *Severe concussion, laceration, mild loss of blood,* the readout said. *Seek medical attention. Recommend 10 mg of perithental-3.*

Concussion. She couldn't have a concussion if she was dead. He switched the display to her vital signs. Her heart rate was low and her breathing was almost nonexistent, but she was alive.

"Lilith," he said, squeezing her shoulder. "Can you hear me?"

She didn't respond. He looked at her screen again. Perithental-3. Was that some kind of stimulant? Maybe the first-aid kit would have some.

"Randall?" he called. "Are you okay?"

Wincing at the pain in his knees and ribs, Michael slid himself through the short neck of the ship and into the main cabin. He braced himself against the wall and panned his headlamp around the room.

He gasped.

The rear of the jumpship was a twisted, mangled wreck. The impact had crushed the starboard side of the ship and split the ship open like a piece of fruit. Randall was leaning back in his seat with a jagged section of the hull protruding from his chest. A frozen froth of blood covered the outside of his suit. His eyes were open and motionless.

Michael clamped his mouth shut and swallowed hard to keep from vomiting. His head swam. He turned away and clutched the back of the copilot's seat with both hands.

"No, no, no," he whispered. Randall couldn't be dead. It wasn't possible. It wasn't fair. Randall had saved their lives. He'd saved Lilith's life. He'd been there just a few moments before, shouting instructions at them. And now he was just a bloody, lifeless corpse.

I killed him, Michael thought. Guilt burned like a fire in his chest. *I killed him, just like I thought I would. I didn't get the calculations right. I didn't start the thrust in time. If I'd been faster, maybe we could have landed safely.*

"I'm sorry," he said. "I'm so sorry." He closed his eyes, but it hardly mattered. The image of Randall's dead body was burned into his brain. Even with his eyes shut, it was all he could see.

"Michael," Lilith whispered.

"I'm here." He blinked away tears and pulled himself back into the cockpit. Lilith looked at him with a glassy expression, as if she didn't quite believe it was him. She coughed twice.

"What happened?" she asked in a faint voice.

"We crashed," Michael said. "Are you okay? How do you feel?"

Lilith made a motion as if to sit up and winced. "My head," she gasped, and settled back into the seat.

"I'll get you some medicine. Stay here."

He looked back down into the cabin. With the starboard side of the ship crumpled inward, there wasn't a lot of room. He crawled to the back of the ship. Randall's body was only an arm's length away. Michael kept his eyes averted. He retrieved the medical kit from its spot on the wall and climbed quickly back up into the cockpit.

"Michael," Lilith said. She still had a dazed expression. "What happened?"

Didn't she remember asking him that just a few minutes before? "We crashed. You hit your head. I've got some medicine."

The first-aid kit had an injector and a case with a dozen plastic ampoules. His eyes fell on the three tubes with lethal doses of pseudomorphine. He shoved them into his pocket and found the perithental. He slid the plastic tube into the injector and held Lilith's arm palm upward.

"This might hurt for a second." He pressed the injector against a small circular port in the suit fabric on her wrist and pulled the trigger. Lilith gasped and pulled her arm away.

"All done," he said. Lilith nodded and closed her eyes. Gently he examined her suit to make sure there were no tears in the fabric, and then he pressed his helmet against hers and inspected the cut on her head. It looked ugly, and it had bled a lot, but it wasn't too deep. He was much more worried about her concussion. *Seek medical attention*, her display still read. How was he supposed to do that?

His first priority was getting himself and Lilith out of the ship. He swung himself down and over to the exterior hatch. He jabbed the open button, but nothing happened. Even the ship's backup power was out. Next to the button was a recessed handle about as long as his arm. Michael slid the handle out until it clicked into place. He rotated it a half turn, and the outer door cracked open. After about a dozen turns, something started to scrape inside the hull and the handle stopped moving. Michael pulled on the handle as hard as he could, but it wouldn't budge. He eyed the opening, which was about half a meter wide. It would have to do. He tossed the bag with their supplies out onto the dusty surface.

Michael slung the rope over his shoulder and started to climb back up to the cockpit. He stopped. It was going to be a lot harder to get Lilith out of the ship if she saw Randall's body. Michael found a thin blanket and covered Randall with it.

He scrambled up to Lilith. She frowned at him. "Michael," she said. "What happened?"

She still didn't remember what had happened, but at least she seemed a little more alert. Maybe the medicine was helping. "We crashed. We need to get out of the ship."

She grimaced. "My head is killing me."

Michael tied the rope around the pilot's seat and tossed the remaining length down into the main cabin. "Grab onto this," he said.

He unfastened her harness and Lilith climbed out of her seat. She held on to the rope with both hands and walked herself down the angled deck and into the main cabin.

"Wow," she said, looking at the damage to the hull. "You weren't kidding."

Michael helped her into the hatchway. She stuck her head through the opening and looked outside. "Where's Randall?"

Michael put his hand on her back and nudged her forward. "I'll explain when we get outside."

Lilith pulled herself back inside and turned toward him. "What do you mean? Where is he?"

"Let's just get outside and—"

But Lilith had already pushed past him and was looking around the mangled cabin. Her headlamp fell on the blanket. "Oh my god."

Michael didn't answer. He reached out for her, but she shook him away.

"Tell me what happened!"

"He didn't make it," Michael said quietly.

Lilith stood frozen for a few moments. "I have to see."

"Lil, I don't think—"

"I have to see him," she said, climbing across the wrecked interior of the ship. She pulled away the blanket. Michael's stomach lurched. From this close, he could see how the fragment of metal had pierced straight through Randall's rib cage. It had been quick, Michael tried to tell himself. He must have died before he even knew what had happened.

"We have to find some way to bury him," Lilith said.

Michael was sure that if Randall were alive, he would have told them in no uncertain terms that they needed to worry about saving themselves first. But he could see that Lilith was determined. He nodded. "Quickly."

They unfastened Randall's harness and wrapped him back up in the blanket. Carefully, they dragged him over to the half-open hatchway. Michael climbed outside, and they pulled Randall inch by inch through the opening until he was lying next to the ship.

Lilith knelt down next to Randall and unwrapped the blanket. The chunk of hull metal that had killed him still protruded from his chest. She rolled him onto his side and worked the fragment back and forth until she'd pulled it free. Michael unclasped Randall's helmet and set it on the ground next to him. Randall's skin was already taut and frozen from the bitterly cold atmosphere. Lilith wiped some of the blood from his mouth and cheeks and closed his eyelids.

He almost looks peaceful, Michael thought. He didn't know what he believed about souls or an afterlife. But he found himself praying that, if there was any such place,

Randall would go there speedily.

Lilith stood up and looked at the fragment of metal in her hand. It was about half a meter long, like a jagged sword without a hilt. She jabbed it into the ground next to Randall's body and started to dig. When Michael realized what she was doing, he climbed into the ship and came out with a shovel.

They dug side by side in the sandy ground until they had a shallow grave, and then they lifted Randall's body and laid him gently inside. Lilith folded his arms across his chest, and they began layering rocks on top of his body. When the last of the rocks had covered his face, they set his helmet on top.

Lilith wrapped her arms around her chest and looked down at the small cairn. "He said he didn't want to dig any more graves. Remember?" Her voice caught in her throat. "He said he'd dug enough already."

Tears were running down her face. Michael realized that he'd never seen her cry before—not even last year when she'd fallen off the top of her house and broken her arm. Crying was such an un-Lilith thing to do.

"I don't ever want to dig another," she said hoarsely.

Michael put his arms around her and hugged her tightly. Which was a very un-Michael thing to do, but right now seemed like the time to make exceptions.

17

ONE EMERGENCY MEDICAL KIT.

One sleeping bag.

Ten meters of nylon rope.

Three pouches of energy gel and six pouches of water.

One lantern.

One shovel.

Michael laid all of the supplies out on the ground next to the ship. It wasn't much. They had some medical supplies and enough food and water to last for a few days. The only good news was that the hull of the ship would protect them from the flare as long as they were careful to stay in the shade. He looked at his wrist screen. About seven hours until sunrise.

How long would it take for them to be rescued? It was possible someone had seen them crash and was on their way right now. But it was also possible that nobody on the entire planet had any idea where they were. They couldn't just wait here until their supplies ran out. Tomorrow night or the night after, they would have to try to make it to Milankovic on their own. It couldn't be more than twenty kilometers away. They should be able to walk there—if everything went well.

"How much longer?" Lilith asked abruptly. She was leaning against the ship with her arms folded, staring off at the horizon with a blank expression.

"Longer?"

"Y' know what I mean," Lilith said. Her voice was a little slurred, as if she'd just woken up from a deep sleep. "Home. How much longer b'fore we go home?"

"I don't know," he said.

Lilith gave an exasperated sigh. "Where's Randall? He'll take me home."

Michael stared at her. "Randall?"

"Yes, *Randall*. Remember him?"

An uneasy feeling settled over Michael. What was Lilith talking about? "Randall is dead," he said carefully.

"Stop lying to me!" she screamed. "He was just here a minute ago."

Michael's mouth went dry. She didn't remember anything about the crash? Something was wrong—something more than just a concussion. He needed to check her suit's medical display.

"Can I look at your wrist screen?" he asked, trying to sound calm.

"No. I need to call my mom." She tapped at her screen and scrolled through various diagnostic displays.

Michael reached out toward her. "Can I just see—"

"No!" she shouted, pulling her arm away. "You always think you're so smart, don't you? You think you've got the answers to everything. Except all you ever really do is mess things up worse."

Michael recoiled. Lilith's face was so twisted with anger that he hardly recognized her.

"Please, Lilith," he said. "Just calm down. We just have to wait here for someone to find us and everything will be okay."

"I'm done waiting. I'm walking home, with or without you."

"Maybe my dad saw us—maybe he'll be here—"

"Oh, will you please *stop* with that already?" She scrunched up her face and stuck out her chin and raised her voice to a mocking falsetto. "All I want to do is drive all night so I can say 'Hi, Dad.' When will you get it through your thick skull that your dad is *gone*? He doesn't care about you. He's moved on."

"That's not true," Michael said hoarsely.

"Go ahead and tell yourself that if it makes you feel any better," she said. "But one of these days you're going to wake up and realize you're on your own."

Her fingers fumbled with the latch mechanism on her collar. "Stupid helmet," she muttered. "I should never have agreed to any of this."

"Lilith, stop!" He tried to grab her, but she pushed him aside. He stumbled and collapsed on the ground. The pain in his ribs, which had faded to a dull throb, flared into agony. He climbed to his hands and knees, heaving for air.

"Why won't it come off?" Lilith growled, pulling at the release clips for her helmet. The collar mechanism, recognizing that the pressure outside the suit was far too low, beeped three times. But it wasn't hard to override the safety features—all she had to do was hold the release latch for ten seconds, and the helmet would unseal from the collar.

"Lilith," he gasped. "Please stop. It's dangerous—the atmosphere—"

"My head is killing me," she said, ignoring him. "If I can just get this stupid thing . . ."

She trailed off. Her hands dropped to her sides, and a confused expression came over her face. "Stupid thing," she said again.

Michael stood up, using the ship to brace himself. "Lilith, something is wrong. Please let me help you."

She looked at him as if she'd just noticed that he was

there, and then her mouth fell open and she slumped down to the ground. A thin, clear fluid ran out of her nose and pooled on the inside of her helmet.

"Lilith!"

Michael knelt down beside her and grabbed her wrist screen. It was flashing a warning: *Probable epidural hematoma. Seek immediate medical attention.*

Michael's head reeled. Seek immediate medical attention . . . or what? Or she could die? He had no idea what an epidural hematoma was. How long did she have? Days? Hours? Minutes?

He rested her head on his lap. *Open your eyes,* he thought. *Please, Lilith, open your eyes. Shout at me, scream at me all you want, but please, open your eyes.*

But Lilith didn't move. Her breathing was so slow and shallow that it almost wasn't there. Sometimes she would pause after exhaling, and Michael would squeeze her hand tightly until she took another breath.

What was he going to do? He couldn't just stay here until someone rescued them. He might survive, but she wouldn't. If he didn't get her to a medical center soon, she would die. He was alone—completely and utterly alone. Cold sweat dripped down the back of his neck. He opened and closed his fists, trying to stave off the panic that he knew was coming.

He couldn't give in. He couldn't. If he didn't keep his

anxiety under control, they would both die out here. But no matter how hard he pushed it away, the black tide in the back of his mind rose higher and higher. He was too exhausted to fight it. The collar of his helmet tightened around his neck like a noose.

"I can't do it," he whispered to Lilith. "You're right. I've messed everything up since the moment we left."

So what? Lilith's voice said inside his head.

The thought surprised him so much that for a moment his rapid breathing stopped. So what? This was all his fault, wasn't it? He was the one who'd gotten Randall killed. He was the one who'd gotten them stranded out here, in the middle of nowhere. He'd made so many mistakes that he could hardly count them all, and the biggest of all had been convincing himself that he was anything other than a failure.

So what?

"I'm the wrong person for this." She needed his father, or his brother, or Randall. She needed someone who knew what they were doing, someone who wasn't going to get her lost or hurt or killed. She needed someone who wasn't going to collapse in a panic attack at the wrong moment. No matter how hard he tried, he wasn't going to be that person.

So what?

He looked down at Lilith's pale face and felt ashamed.

Lilith didn't have anyone else. All she had was him. She'd come on this trip just because she'd wanted to help him. Now she needed him, and he was worrying about whether he was the right person? He was the *only* person.

He had to do this. Nothing else mattered. He could fail at everything he did for the rest of his life as long as he got this one thing right.

Gradually the black panic faded away until it was just a dull cloud in the back of his mind. His muscles unclenched and his breathing slowed. Anxiety was his brain's way of keeping him safe, wasn't that what his doctor had said? Well, right now there was something more important than keeping himself safe. He wasn't going to just sit here and wait for his best friend to take her last breath. He was going to find a way to get her home.

He laid her head down gently and stood up. His first problem was figuring out exactly where they were. He sighted half a dozen stars and began plotting their position. It was the same process he'd followed during the suit test, except that this time, their lives depended on him getting it right. He worked carefully, and in about ten minutes he had six overlapping arcs. The good news was that the area in the middle was small enough that he had a pretty accurate idea of where they were. The bad news was that it showed Milankovic was almost twenty kilometers away.

His heart sank. Twenty kilometers. Could he make it that far before the sun came up? He might be able to lug her on his shoulders for few hundred meters, but there was no way he'd be able to carry her all the way to Milankovic by himself. He needed a stretcher or a litter—something that would slide over the ground smoothly and help him conserve his strength.

Michael poked through the wreckage of the ship until he found a large, curved piece of the engine cowling that had snapped off. He leaned it against a rock and lifted Lilith onto it. It held her in a half-reclined position like a big bucket seat. He took the length of rope and tied her to the makeshift stretcher and looped the ends over his shoulders. He leaned forward and pulled. His ribs yelped in pain. It took more effort than he expected, but it would work.

"Okay," he said. "Let's get moving."

18

TWENTY KILOMETERS. TWO minutes in a jumpship; a half hour in a rover; five hours on foot.

Michael searched for the spot between the constellations Cygnus and Cepheus that indicated due north. *On Earth, we had it easy,* he remembered his dad saying. *Nice, bright Polaris. Mars likes to make things hard.*

He wrapped the ends of the rope under his arms and started forward.

By the time he'd gone a few hundred meters, his back and shoulders were already knotted and sore. It was hard enough dragging the stretcher over sand and dirt, where it left a wide furrow like an old-fashioned plow, but whenever it hit even the smallest rock, Michael was jerked to a stop. He wound his way left and right, trying to stay on a clear path, which made him feel like he was walking two kilometers for every one he moved in a straight line.

You have no idea where you are, a voice said in his head. *Following the stars? How well has that worked out for you before?*

He clenched his jaw and bent forward, trying to block the voice from his head.

Nobody is looking for you. Nobody cares.

"Stop," he whispered.

Why are you even doing this? the voice asked. *She's as good as dead. Now you're going to die too, out here in the middle of nowhere, all alone.*

"Stop!" The sound of his voice startled him. He looked back at Lilith, slumped over with her head on her chest. He could see the slow rise and fall of her shoulders as she breathed. He tightened the rope around his torso and started walking again.

After two hours, he took a short break to work out the kinks in his shoulders and legs and take a drink of water. When he picked up the ropes again and looked at the stars, he had trouble finding the right constellations. Everything looked different. Many stars weren't visible at all, and even the brilliant blue-white of Sirius was pale and muted. What was going on?

The wind gusted and dust swirled around him. His mouth dropped open as he realized what was happening. The dust storm was spreading off the ice cap and across the northern plain, and it had finally caught up to him here. And as it grew denser, it was blocking out the stars.

Blocking out the only chance he had of finding his way back home.

He started to walk quickly. How long did he have before the sky was completely black? The thought terrified him, and not only because he wouldn't have any means of navigation. The vast spread of stars didn't illuminate very much, but it was a reassuring, familiar glow. To lose all of that, to be out on the surface alone underneath a pitch-black sky . . .

Cepheus was already down to just three stars. Several other constellations had disappeared completely. As he watched, a dark cloud swept overhead, and the tail of Cygnus flickered and disappeared.

Dust floated all around him like water. Soon the beam from his headlamp was like a solid cone of light that bobbed up and down. The muscles in his legs burned. All he could see of Cygnus was the faint glow of Deneb. A few moments later, even that was gone, and the sky was an empty, inky-gray void.

The sea of dust seemed to weigh on his shoulders, pressing him down toward the ground. The stars were gone. How could he make it to Milankovic now? He had no way of telling which way he was supposed to go. Everything around him looked the same. He tried to focus on the path he'd been following, but after only a few minutes his sense of direction faded and he had no idea which way he was going.

A distant beeping caught his attention. It was barely audible over the labored sound of his breathing. Where was it coming from? He looked at his wrist screen, but it didn't show any warnings.

The beeping grew louder. He turned and looked at Lilith. Her screen was flashing bright red: *Carbon dioxide levels dangerously high.*

What was going on? Had there been some damage to her suit during the crash? A problem with her filter, or her respirator? He examined her wrist screen's diagnostics. It was reporting that her air filter had become saturated and it was no longer converting the CO_2 in her suit to oxygen. But how could that have happened? When he'd checked their filters before they left the homestead, both of them had had weeks of life left.

He unwrapped the ropes that held Lilith to the stretcher and gently rolled her onto her stomach. The filter was built into the collar of her suit, just between her shoulder blades. In the glow of his headlamp, he could see a hairline crack in the casing. He opened the outer cover and saw that the crack extended down into the air unit itself. It must have been damaged during the crash. Ever since then, CO_2 from the atmosphere had been leaking into the filter, until finally its trillions of molecular sieves were full. Now every breath that Lilith took was filling her bloodstream with lethal carbon dioxide.

He emptied the first-aid kit onto the ground. There was a single spare filter. He popped out the filter on her air unit and swapped it for the fresh one. He sat down next to her and watched the CO_2 levels in her suit drop down slowly.

But the real problem hadn't been with her filter—it was the crack in her air unit. In an hour or two, the new filter would be saturated as well, and carbon dioxide would build up in her suit again. CO_2 poisoning was bad enough for someone who was healthy and awake. For Lilith, it could be fatal.

He had to switch their air units, so that she had the working one. Hot-swapping was dangerous in the best of conditions. Doing it by yourself, in the dark, for the very first time . . .

But there weren't any other options.

Michael knelt down next to Lilith and turned up the oxygen levels in his own suit as high as they would go. He counted thirty deep breaths and disconnected his air unit from the ports on his collar.

His suit buzzed a loud warning. He unsnapped his air unit and set it on the ground. Every second of oxygen was vital, and he needed to do this quickly. But it was a complicated process, and it took him almost a minute to get everything switched over. Finally, he snapped the working assembly back into her suit's collar and hooked up the intake and exhaust ports. By the time Lilith's suit was fully reconnected, his own suit was flashing a warning: *Oxygen levels nearly depleted.*

He didn't have much time. He fumbled with the connections on the back of his suit. There was no point in breathing anymore; all of the oxygen in his suit was gone. He could hear the blood rushing in his ears. Why wouldn't the hoses reconnect properly? Everything around him was turning red.

He stared at Lilith's collar. His brain ticked slowly and every thought took enormous effort. Hoses. There were two hoses, one for supplying oxygen and one for removing carbon dioxide. . . .

He'd been trying to jam the wrong hoses into the wrong ports. He swapped them, and they clicked into place. He took a deep breath but got nothing. He tried again and again. He could feel his lungs expanding and contracting, but it was as if they were disconnected from the rest of his body. His heart was being squeezed by an invisible fist. His eyes struggled to focus.

this is what dying feels like

A wisp of oxygen snaked into his chest. Then another, and another. The air was cold and bitter. He took long, gasping breaths, each one deeper than the last, until his lungs ached with the sheer joy of breathing.

Michael sat next to Lilith and looked out into the darkness.

The air in her suit was clean, and the carbon dioxide levels in her bloodstream were back to normal. Now his worry was his own air supply. He was wearing the damaged unit, which meant that soon his own filter would be saturated and CO_2 would start to build up in his blood.

He remembered Randall talking about the symptoms of carbon dioxide poisoning: headaches, vomiting, hallucinations. It had all sounded so horrible at the time, but now his only concern was how far he'd be able to go before he collapsed. He knew their chances of making it all the way to the colony were slim. But if they could get close, then maybe someone would find them. And maybe he would still be alive when that happened.

Maybe. But not very likely. He pulled the ampoules of pseudomorphine out of his pocket and stared at them. Randall was right: radiation poisoning was a horrible way to die. If they were still out here when the sun rose . . .

"Michael."

The sound of Lilith's voice, even in such a low whisper, made him jump. She was looking at him through half-open eyes. He squeezed her hand.

"How are you feeling?" he asked.

"Awful." She exhaled slowly, as if speaking took more energy than she could muster.

"We're going to be okay. We're almost home. Just a little while longer."

Lilith looked at him for a long moment. The corners of her mouth curled up into the faintest of smiles. "You're still a terrible liar," she said, and closed her eyes.

He bit his lip. His breath hissed through his nostrils. For several minutes he watched the slow rise and fall of her chest. Then he climbed to his feet and picked up the rope harness.

"You're going to be okay," he said again, and set off into the darkness.

Without any stars to guide him, he didn't know the exact direction of Milankovic, so all he could do was try to keep going in a straight line. The voice at the back of his head laughed grimly. Even with the stars, he'd only had the vaguest of ideas where he was going. What were his chances of getting there now, wandering blindly across the surface of Mars?

When he'd walked a few kilometers, his suit flashed

a CO_2 warning. The air in his helmet tasted thick and metallic. Soon he had a throbbing headache, as if his brain was trying to burst out of his skull.

After a while—three minutes? thirty minutes?—he was forced to stop again. His arms and legs felt as if they were buried in sand. He sat down and drank one of the water pouches. The random flickering pattern of dust floating in the beam of his headlamp was hypnotizing, and a warm drowsiness settled over him.

He couldn't fall asleep. If he fell asleep, he might not ever wake up. But surely he could rest here for a minute. Just for a minute. Then he would start walking again.

As his eyelids sagged shut, he saw a faint light in the darkness ahead. He snapped awake. His heart thumped in his chest. He saw it again: the yellow glow of a headlamp bobbing up and down in the darkness.

"Hello?" he shouted. His throat burned with the effort. "Hello!"

There was no response. The light started to move away from him.

"Wait!" He grabbed the harness and struggled to pull Lilith toward the light. But his legs didn't have any strength, and he couldn't manage anything more than a slow, torturous walk. The light faded and disappeared.

"Stop!" he screamed.

Michael turned and looked back at Lilith. He couldn't

leave her here. He might never find her again. But whoever that was out in the darkness, he had to reach them before it was too late.

"I'm sorry," he said, kneeling next to Lilith. Tears streamed down his face. "I'll be back. I promise. I'll be back no matter what."

He stumbled off in the direction of the light. His lungs weren't getting enough oxygen, but adrenaline pushed him on. He moved clumsily through the darkness. Twenty meters, then thirty, then forty. He stopped and turned off his own headlamp and held his breath, watching and listening for any sign of the other person.

"Help us!" he screamed. His voice was swallowed up in the blackness. "Please help us!"

The wind shifted, and for a moment a yellow light winked at him, like a star shining in the darkness. As quickly as it had appeared, it was gone again, leaving a faint afterglow burned into his retina. He kept his headlamp off and staggered forward. Every step was slow and difficult, as if the dust in the air were physically holding him back. He didn't dare take his eyes off the spot where the light had appeared. He told himself over and over that it had been real, that it hadn't been just a reflection in his helmet or a figment of his imagination. But no matter how far he walked or how long he stared, the light didn't reappear.

He screamed at himself. Couldn't he go any faster? There wasn't anything left to do but run so *run run run*

After only a few meters he tripped and fell hard. *Get up,* he thought, but his foot was caught on something. He squinted and pulled at his leg and saw that he'd tripped over a pipe that ran along the ground.

A pipe.

A metal pipe.

19

MICHAEL STARED AT the pipe. Was it really there? He kicked it and it made a hollow metal thunk. It was real enough. It had been buried about half a meter below the surface, but erosion had formed a little gully, exposing a short section that was barely big enough to catch his foot. If he'd been running just a little ways to either side, he would have passed it by without even knowing it was there.

What was the pipe for? Where did it lead? It was about ten centimeters across, and the metal had been wrapped with a thin layer of heating fabric. He could feel the warmth through his glove. *Water*, he thought. It was a water pipe. Which meant one direction or the other led to Milankovic.

His heart thumped in his chest. He climbed up out of the gully and gauged the direction of the pipe. He walked in a careful, straight line, putting one foot in front of the other to make sure he didn't wander to one side or the other. After a few dozen meters, a dome-shaped building emerged from the darkness. In the swirling dust it looked ghostly and unreal. It was about the size of his house back in Heimdall, with a single door and a sign that read Milankovic Water Authority. The pipe reemerged from the ground and met up with a complicated-looking series of valves and gauges connecting several pipes at the rear of the building.

Out of the corner of his eye, he saw something moving in the darkness. He turned and saw the person with the yellow headlamp standing a few meters away. Relief and joy flooded over Michael. "Hello," he said, fumbling for words. "Thank you—I was lost. My friend and I were lost."

The person didn't reply. Something was wrong with their suit. Other than the yellow headlamp, none of their lights or displays were on—not even the basic green status lights that indicated power and pressure. Michael shone his headlamp at the person's face.

It was Randall.

Michael screamed. Randall's artificial eyes, frozen

over with blue-white ice, stared back at him with an empty expression. His ribs protruded from his chest like bony fingers, and his suit was spattered with blood.

This couldn't be happening. Randall was dead. They had buried him. He was *dead*.

"No," Michael said, sagging down onto the ground.

No, said Randall, and took a few steps toward him.

Terror gripped Michael. "You can't be here," he said. He held out his hand as if to ward Randall off. "It's not my fault!"

Fault.

"Leave me alone!"

Alone, Randall said. He was almost an arm's length away from Michael now. Michael could see his heart beating inside his chest, squeezing and relaxing in slow, halting beats.

Anger welled up inside Michael. This wasn't possible. "You aren't real!" he screamed.

Randall kept walking forward. Michael backed up until his shoulders were pressed up against the door to the station. "My name is Michael Prasad. My mother is Laura and my father is Manish and you're not real!"

Real, Randall said. He stopped and looked at Michael warily.

"Mars is six thousand seven hundred seventy-eight kilometers in diameter," Michael said. The words rushed out of him in one long breath. "The molecular weight of carbon is twelve point oh one oh seven. The speed of light is two hundred ninety-nine million seven hundred ninety-two thousand four hundred fifty-eight meters per second and *you are not real*!"

Real, Randall repeated. He reached out with a blood-spattered glove. It moved toward Michael until the tip of his index finger was almost touching Michael's helmet. Michael closed his eyes.

"I tried," he whispered. "I did everything I could."

He held his breath and waited. The only sound was the beating of his heart in his chest. When he opened his eyes again, Randall was gone.

Michael stared at the spot where Randall had been standing just moments ago. He told himself that it had just been a hallucination, but his body wouldn't stop shaking. He put his hand against the door of the pumping station to steady himself, and then he staggered inside.

Overhead lights flickered on, and he squinted at the sudden brightness. Most of the space in the station was taken up by a huge pumping apparatus. The pump rumbled as it worked, making the entire station tremble. A variety of pipes connected the pump to the pipe junctions next to the door. On the other side of the room, a set of shelves held everything from tiny screwdrivers to pipe segments as big as his legs. Next to the door, a portable screen with several multicolored wires trailing out of it sat on a plastic rolling cart.

Michael winced at the stabbing pain in his head. He didn't have much longer before the CO_2 poisoning killed him. He searched through the shelves for spare air filters. A wave of dizziness and nausea hit him, and he stumbled into the plastic cart. The cart toppled over, scattering pieces of equipment across the floor. A thumb-sized magnet rolled toward the pump's casing and attached itself with a sharp *thunk*.

His wrist screen was flashing wildly. The carbon dioxide in his suit had reached nearly lethal levels. He crawled across the floor on his hands and knees, breathing heavily. He found a box and emptied it. Cans of lubricants, sealants, and other chemicals. Nothing he could use. Something red caught his eye: an emergency kit. He grabbed it and dug through suit patches and flares and splints. At the bottom of the case he found two white plastic cylinders. He had to squint at them before he realized what they were: replacement filters.

Michael twisted his collar around until he could reach his air unit. His fingers were stiff and cold. He opened the filter compartment, jerked out the old filter, and snapped a new one into place.

He leaned back against the pump casing. He could feel the hum of the machinery inside. He was tired. So tired. His eyes slid closed.

Michael was lying on his bed at home. It was morning, and bright sunlight was shining through the window. The tree in the yard outside rustled quietly.

His mom was sitting on the bed next to him. She was smiling and holding her hand against his head. His dad leaned in the doorway with his hands in his pockets. His eyes were deep and somber and Michael couldn't tell if he was angry, or sad, or disappointed, or a mixture of all three.

"Did someone find us?" Michael asked. "Where's Lilith?"

Michael's mom kept smiling. She ran her fingers through his hair as if she hadn't heard him.

"Please, tell me how Lilith is." He tried to sit up. "Is she okay?"

His mom's smile disappeared. She looked at him sadly and shook her head.

"No," he said. "That's not possible."

Michael looked at his father, who still hadn't moved. Michael was struck with a sudden terror. *Please don't say anything,* he thought. *Please.*

His dad opened his mouth to speak. His tongue and the inside of his mouth were black. His teeth were yellow and rotten.

Michael screamed.

He sat up with a jerk, kicking his legs and sending the emergency kit sliding across the floor. The sound of his breathing echoed in his helmet. He looked at his wrist screen. The filter was working: the carbon dioxide in his suit had dropped down to a safe level. Not that he needed his suit diagnostics to tell him that: if the filter hadn't been working, he would never have woken up again.

He put his hand on the pump and stood slowly. His head still throbbed with pain. He followed the pump around and found a control panel with several gauges and readouts, none of which made any sense to him. Below the gauges was a red-handled lever and a small printed sign. In Case of Emergency, Please Notify R. Weiss Immediately.

Impulsively, Michael pulled the lever. The rumbling of the motor slowed, and the readings on the gauges dropped. When they reached zero, the pump shuddered to a stop. The light on the control panel turned red.

Somewhere in Milankovic, the water pressure from this pipe would be dropping. How long would it take for someone to notice? Michael wondered if R. Weiss was going to be happy about getting that call.

Lilith, he reminded himself. *You have to find Lilith.* She was still out there somewhere.

Michael stood in the doorway and looked out into the darkness. The blackish-red dust was like a wall of static. How was he going to find her? He didn't have the vaguest notion of which direction he'd been coming from when he stumbled over the pipe. And how far had he run? Twenty meters? Fifty? A hundred? It had all blurred together.

And when he did find Lilith—how was he going to find his way back? Visibility was so bad that he could pass right by the station without knowing. He needed a way to navigate in the darkness.

"Lilith!" he screamed, more from frustration than anything else. Even if she was awake, she was too far away to hear him.

He sat down in the doorway. *Think*, he told himself. *You need a plan. How to find Lilith, and how to find your way back.*

An idea came to him. He thought a little more, turning it over in his head. Yes, it could work. He'd seen what he needed inside the station. But it was risky.

Maybe someone will find me here soon, he thought.

Maybe there's a big search party on its way now. They'll find me, and they'll find Lilith, and we'll both be safe.

Maybe. It was possible. But he didn't have time to wait around. If Lilith was still out there when the sun came up, she wouldn't last long. He had to find her and get her to Milankovic as soon as possible.

You have your plan, he told himself. *Now do it.*

He turned and went into the station and found the emergency kit. He counted out the flares: sixteen of them, wrapped together like a bundle of magic wands. He stuffed them into the pockets of his suit and went back outside. He took one flare and snapped off one end. A bright spark like a miniature star appeared where he had broken it.

He set off into the darkness, counting his steps carefully. After fifty steps he turned and looked back. He could just barely make out the lights in the doorway of the station. He jammed the flare into the ground so that the burning part stuck up like a flag, and then he used his finger to draw an arrow in the dirt pointing back toward the station. He set out more flares every fifty steps until he had four of them laid out in a straight line that led all the way back to the pumping station.

One direction covered. He followed the flares back to the doorway and set out three more lines at ninety degrees from each other, so that the flares formed a gigantic cross with the pumping station at the center.

He took a deep breath. Now he was ready. In theory, as long as he didn't wander too far from the station, he would eventually see one of the flares, and he could follow his way back.

In theory.

He walked in a slow curve, keeping the station to his left. When he'd gone a hundred steps, and he still hadn't seen the next flare, he started to get frantic. Could it already have burned out? If his plan didn't work, he'd be wandering out here until his air filter became saturated again and the CO_2 in his suit killed him.

Michael turned off his headlamp and closed his eyes for a few seconds. Then he looked out into the darkness and turned in a slow circle.

There—behind him and to his right. He'd gone right past the flare without noticing. He found the arrow he'd drawn in the sand and reoriented himself. It was scary how easy it was to lose your sense of direction in the darkness.

That's why you have the flares, he told himself. *Now keep going. Lilith is still out here somewhere.*

He walked in a wider arc toward the next row of markers and found the flare a little to the left of where he'd expected it. He adjusted again, and found the third and fourth arms of the cross.

Now he was back where he'd started. One of his three circles was complete, and he hadn't gotten lost. Of course, he hadn't seen any sign of Lilith, either, which meant that she was farther out from the station. He tried not to think about the possibility that she was so far away that his flares wouldn't even reach her.

The second and third rings were more difficult than the first. The distances between the sets of flares were longer, and it was harder to follow the right arc. He passed by each of the flares without seeing it and had to double back. On one segment, he had to backtrack three times before he finally found the marker.

He moved out to the last ring. The flares were starting to burn down. How long would they last? He walked quickly. This time, there were over three hundred steps between each flare. He missed the first and second flares by wide margins and had to spend precious time searching, tracing ever-widening circles until he found them.

Michael was so focused on keeping himself from getting lost that he almost missed Lilith.

20

WHEN MICHAEL SAW a yellow gleam in the darkness to his right, about a hundred steps outside the outermost circle, he was so intent on finding the next flare that he ignored it for a moment. After a few seconds, something clicked in his brain and he realized what he'd seen.

"Lilith!" he shouted, running through the swirling brown fog. She was still slumped over on the stretcher with her eyes closed. A fine layer of red dust covered her suit. He was lucky to have found her—five meters farther away, and he would never have seen the light from her headlamp. He grabbed her wrist screen and checked her vital signs. She was alive, but her breathing and heart rate had slowed even further.

He'd done it. He'd found her. Now all he had to do

was get her back to the pumping station, and then . . . what? He pushed that thought away. He'd figure it out when they got there.

"Come on," Michael said. He picked up the ropes and wrapped them around his chest. Which way? He tried to reconstruct it all in his mind—the flares, the station, the place where he'd found Lilith. *That way*, he decided, focusing his eyes on a particular spot in the darkness ahead. The station should be no more than two hundred steps away, and with any luck he'd see one of his flares and it would guide him back.

Pulling Lilith was harder than he'd remembered. The replacement filter he'd installed was getting saturated, and his head throbbed painfully. He suddenly realized that he'd left the last spare filter back at the station. If he couldn't find his way back soon, that mistake was going to kill him.

After a dozen meters, he was already panting for air. Lilith's stretcher felt like an anchor digging into the ground. Fifty steps, then a hundred, but there was no sign of the station or any of the flares. When he got to two hundred steps, he turned off his lamp and closed his eyes for a minute and then scanned the darkness. Nothing. Not a speck of light anywhere.

When he'd gone three hundred steps, he stopped. Somehow he'd missed the station. His chest tightened with panic. *It's okay,* he told himself. He just had to pick another angle and try again, and he was bound to find the station eventually.

Eventually. He didn't have time for *eventually.* The pain in his head was making it difficult to concentrate. His mind drifted off into a hazy, cold emptiness. At some point he tripped and fell. He stayed on his hands and knees for a moment, staring at the ground, trying to remember what he'd been doing. His mind snapped awake, and he looked back the way he'd come. How far since he'd turned around? Two hundred steps? Three hundred? He couldn't remember.

He was lost. All of that preparation, and it hadn't helped at all. He was lost and had no idea how to get back.

Michael took a deep breath. One more time. He'd turn back one more time, and then he was done. He pushed himself to his feet and turned Lilith around. He had no idea where the station was, but it didn't really matter. Pick a direction and go. Keep going until you can't anymore.

When he'd gone another hundred steps, he saw something on the ground ahead of him. A white line of dust, like chalk. He squinted at it. After a moment he realized that it was the burned-out husk of a flare. Only the tiniest spark remained at one end.

Now what? he thought dully. He found the arrow he'd drawn in the dirt and followed it with his eyes. The station. The station was that way.

He set off again. He tried to count his steps, but his head hurt too much. It was all he could do to keep going in a straight line. After what seemed like an eternity, he saw the yellow glow of the station's lights.

"We're there, Lil," he panted. For a moment he thought that this was part of Milankovic, somewhere with people, somewhere they would be safe. Then he remembered. This was just a remote pumping station outside the main colony. They weren't safe at all.

He pulled her through the door, squinting in the fluorescent light. He let the ropes drop and grabbed the emergency kit. One more air filter. He pulled out the old one and slid the replacement into its place.

He looked at his wrist screen. How long had the previous filter lasted? An hour? Maybe less? The crack in his air unit must be getting worse. He didn't have much time left.

Michael's eyes fell on the pipe that led from the pump machinery and out through the wall. That pipe went to Milankovic. All he needed was a way to follow it. He stood up. His skull still pulsed with pain, but the oxygen from the new filter was already helping his mind to clear. He needed to take advantage of that clarity now, because it wasn't going to last long.

He went outside and around to where the pipe left the building. It ran along the ground for a few meters and then dipped below the surface. If he could follow the pipe, he could reach the colony. But he'd already seen how difficult it was to keep to a straight line for more than a few minutes in this empty darkness.

He traced the pipe with his fingers. It felt like solid steel. How deep was it buried? Was there was a way to follow it even if he couldn't see it?

Michael ran back inside and found the plastic cart he'd knocked over earlier. He grabbed a spool of insulated electrical wire and cut off a piece about a meter long. He searched the ground around the cart. He knew he'd seen it—a metal cylinder like a squat tube of toothpaste. . . .

There, stuck to the pump casing. He pried the magnet off and attached it to the wire with some electrical tape. He ran back outside and dangled it over the ground. When the magnet passed over the buried pipe, the wire jerked taut, like an invisible dog pulling at a leash. With a little experimentation, he found that if he held the magnet at the right height, he could use it to follow the path of the pipe.

Now he knew how to find the colony. All that was left was to get there. He ran back to Lilith. "Okay. This is it. The last little bit, and then we're finished."

He held her hand tightly for a few moments, hoping

maybe her eyes would open, but she remained motionless. He stood up and wrapped the ropes of the harness around his chest and pulled her out to where the pipe disappeared into the ground. He walked quickly, holding the wire with the magnet out in front of him. Time was the most important thing, now. In a little while the last air filter would be saturated and the carbon dioxide would build up in his body again. He had to get as far as he could before . . .

Before what?

Before he started seeing more ghosts. Before he collapsed. Before he died.

Michael's vision faded until the only thing he saw was the ground right in front of him. He felt like he was on an enormous treadmill, walking through the same landscape over and over again. Twice he wandered too far from the pipe and had to spend a panicked minute searching for it. If he hadn't had the magnet to guide him, he would have been wandering in circles.

Or maybe he was wandering in circles anyway.

After half an hour, he stopped to drink some water and suck down some energy gel. He took a few deep breaths and looked back at Lilith, and then he started walking again. How much farther? Five kilometers? Ten? It didn't really matter. He wasn't going to make it. Everything had gotten so simple. He just needed to walk until he couldn't walk any farther. One step, and then another, and then another. At some point there would be no more steps to take, and he would be done.

The headache came back first, and then the shortness of breath. His last air filter was finally saturated. Without any warning, his stomach clenched and he threw up. Vomit dribbled down the inside of his suit and onto his chest. He swished some water around in his mouth and kept going. After that he lost track of how many times he stopped to rest. Everything blended together. He had always been out here, and he always would be. His suit blared various warnings at him until he finally tore off his wrist screen and left it on the ground.

The sky had started to brighten when he finally stumbled and fell. He tried a few times to push himself to his feet, but he didn't have the strength. This was it. This was as far as he could go.

He lay on his back, looking up at the sky. The sun was going to come up soon. At least they weren't going to die in total darkness. And really, this wasn't such a bad spot. It was sandy and comfortable. A warm, tingly numbness spread through his arms and legs. These suits were the best coffins ever made—wasn't that what Randall had said? It had scared him then, but now it seemed reassuring.

He reached out and rested his hand on Lilith's helmet. She was still breathing. She was still alive. He'd done what he'd set out to do. The rest didn't really matter anymore.

The sun slowly climbed over the horizon. The dust around them glowed a warm, peaceful red. Shapes flickered at the edge of his vision like candle flames. They marched toward him and back away in slow cycles, each time creeping a little bit nearer. It felt odd not to have to worry about what would happen when they finally reached him.

One of the shapes separated itself from the rest. It began shouting and running toward him. He tried to tell them that they had won, that Mars had beaten him. It was okay. The shapes surrounded him, and he felt himself being lifted up and cradled like a child. *Michael,* a voice said, warm and gentle and familiar: *Michael, Michael, Michael.* A man's face pressed up against his until it was separated only by the thin plastic of their helmets.

"Hi, Dad," Michael murmured, and then closed his eyes.

21

THE EARLY-MORNING LIGHT filtering into the lobby of the medical center shimmered on the polished granite floor. Michael sat on a bench with his arms wrapped around his knees and stared through the glass doors at the plaza outside. A woman setting out flowers in the gift shop gave him a warm smile. She'd seen him here so often over the last few weeks that she probably wondered if he had an actual home.

"Is your friend leaving today?" the woman asked.

"Yes," Michael said. "At least, that's what they told me."

The woman walked over and set down a small flowerpot with a single white orchid on the bench next to him. "For her."

"Oh, you don't have to do that," Michael said, trying to hand the orchid back to her.

"Please, take it."

Michael followed her back toward the shop, holding the flowerpot out in front of him. "No, I can't, really. And anyway I don't know if she even likes—"

He stopped midsentence and turned around as the doors to the elevator slid open and an attendant pushed Lilith in a wheelchair out into the lobby, followed by Lilith's mother.

"It wasn't my legs that were hurt, it was my head," Lilith was saying. "I'm telling you, I don't have any problems walking."

"And miss, I'm telling you that it's our policy," the attendant said.

"Dumb policy. Waste of time."

"In this case, I completely agree." The attendant tapped something into her screen.

"Lilith, give the woman a break," her mother said in a tired voice. "Look, you have a welcoming party. Hello, Michael."

"Hello, Ms. Colson."

"Is that for me?" Lilith asked, eyeing the flower with an amused expression.

Michael looked down at the flowerpot in his hands. Blood rushed to his cheeks as he tried to stammer a reply. He turned to hand it back to the woman, but she had already disappeared back into her shop.

"Of course it's for you," her mother said, taking the

flower from Michael and handing it to Lilith. "It's very pretty."

"Thank you," Lilith said. Her eyes glinted at Michael's obvious discomfort. "That was very . . . thoughtful."

"Well, I'll give you two a minute," her mom said. She gave Michael a kiss on the cheek, which made his blush deepen. "We'll be waiting outside."

"Can I please stand up now?" Lilith asked the attendant as her mother walked out through the doors of the medical center.

The attendant helped her out of the wheelchair. "Please be careful. We wouldn't want you to have to come back for another stay anytime soon."

Lilith yawned and stretched her neck and shoulders. She held the orchid up to the light. "Did you really get this for me?"

"Well—no, not exactly," Michael said.

"Good," she said. "I was starting to get worried."

There was an awkward silence. He put his hands into his pockets and pulled them back out again. *Hypothesis: sometimes telling the truth is much, much harder than lying.*

"There's something I want to tell you," he said. "A few things, actually. But don't say anything until I'm done, okay? Because I had to practice this and I don't want to mess it up."

"Okay," Lilith said, a little uncertainly.

"First, that I think you're right, and I wouldn't know a girlfriend if one punched me in the face."

"Exactly!" she blurted out, and then put her hand over her mouth. "Sorry. Keep going."

"Second, that I don't know anyone that I like anywhere near as much as you. You're pretty incredible."

At the word "incredible," Lilith raised her eyebrow, but kept quiet. He took a deep breath and went on.

"Third, that waiting for you to come out of surgery was ten times harder than anything I'd ever done. And that it seems like anytime you're someplace, that's where I want to be, and that whenever you're not someplace where I am, I want you to stop not being there. . . ."

Michael trailed off. His heart was beating so quickly, he could have been in the middle of a panic attack. "Okay, so I guess that was either four or five things, depending on how you want to count."

Lilith stared at him with wide-eyed astonishment. For a long moment, she seemed speechless. "I hope you don't think you can tell someone all of that and expect them to be able to *answer*."

"I guess I just wanted to tell you," he mumbled. "You don't really need to say anything."

"Of course I don't need to say anything!" she said, throwing up her hands. "Anyone with half a brain would have figured it out by now."

"Figured out what?"

"That *I'm* the one who told Marcy Dagher that I've had a crush on you since fifth grade!" she shouted.

He stared at her. Suddenly six different things she'd said to him all made sense, all at the same time. He opened his mouth to speak before realizing that he didn't have the slightest clue of what to say. "Oh," he finally managed.

"And that was before you saved my life by dragging me twenty kilometers through the middle of a dust storm with a broken air unit and two cracked ribs. So don't talk to *me* about incredible."

Before he could answer, she jabbed a finger at him. "But this doesn't mean you can go around telling everyone I'm your girlfriend now. Got it?"

"Okay," Michael said, a little bewildered.

"On the other hand, if I ever hear you tell anyone I'm *not* your girlfriend, there's an excellent chance that you really will get punched in the face." She said this thoughtfully, as if she were describing an allergic reaction that she didn't quite understand. "So it's probably best if we just take the word 'girlfriend' off the table for a while. Deal?"

Michael tried to piece together what she was saying. *Hypothesis confirmed: sometimes girls really do say things just to confuse you.* "Deal," he said, shaking her hand.

"Hey," Lilith said, as if something had just occurred to her. "Why did my mom say that *we'll* be waiting outside? Did someone from our class show up? Please tell me it wasn't Marcy. I really don't think I could look her in the eye right now."

"No," Michael said. "It's not Marcy."

"So who is it?" Lilith asked, peering through the doors at the plaza outside. "No way it's Gwen Mackenzie. She's still mad at me for—"

Suddenly she stopped. Her face froze in an expression of shock. She looked at Michael and then back out at the plaza, where a tall man with dark hair was pacing back and forth.

"He's here?" she said. "She *called* him?"

"Well, not exactly," Michael said. "But she did give me his address."

Now wasn't the right time to tell Lilith that it had taken days of pleading before her mother had even agreed to *that*. He also didn't really need to pass on any of the unique and colorful adjectives her mother had used to describe her ex-husband, some of which Michael had needed to look up in a dictionary. The important thing was that Lilith's dad was out there on the plaza, waiting for her to come out of the hospital.

"And he actually came?" Lilith said.

"I barely had time to tell him that you were in the

hospital before he'd booked a ticket. I honestly didn't think it was possible to get here from Earth that quickly."

Lilith was quiet for a moment. "It's not like this fixes everything. He's still been a jerk."

"Yeah," Michael said. "But it's a start, right?"

"I don't even know what to say to him."

"Well," he said, "you can start with 'Hi, Dad.' That's worked pretty well for me in the past."

She nodded but still didn't move. "Are you okay?" Michael asked.

"Sure," she said. "I just need to figure out how to go out there and talk to my dad, which ought to be the most normal thing in the world to do. But first . . ."

She leaned toward him and her lips pressed against his cheek. Before he even realized what was happening, it was over. He stood completely motionless as a warm flush spread over his face. She'd kissed him. Hadn't she? It had definitely met all the basic criteria for a kiss. . . .

"Thank you," she said.

"For what?" he said, blinking. "I mean—sure. Of course. You're welcome."

She straightened up and squared her shoulders. "All right. Let's do this. But later, you and me need to plan out where we're going next."

"Going next?" he asked. "Like on some kind of trip?"

"Exactly," she said, pushing open the door. "Except

this time, no dust storms, explosions, or solar flares."

She glanced back at him, her eyes sparkling. "See, I've always wanted to visit Saturn. . . ."

Michael pressed his forehead against the colony dome and watched as a big passenger jumpship fell in from the upper atmosphere, leaving a white trail like a shooting star. It braked to a stop a hundred meters above the Martian surface, and then it settled down onto an empty landing pad.

"That's my ship," his dad said from behind him.

Michael nodded. The ship's gangway descended, and a few of the other passengers, who were already suited up and waiting near the landing pad, climbed aboard.

Michael was standing with his family in a little plaza near one of the colony's main passenger airlocks. A voice over a loudspeaker announced that the shuttle to Milankovic was now boarding. A crew of technicians started loading crates of equipment into the airlock.

"How long do you think it will take to rebuild the station?" Peter asked.

"It'll be months before it's completely ready," their dad said. "But we're hoping to get the magnetic field back up in a couple of weeks. The astronomers are saying there's virtually zero chance of another flare anytime soon, but we're not taking any chances."

"Where are you going to be staying until the station is rebuilt?" their mom asked.

"Actually, there's a little homestead not too far away," he said, smiling. "I think Michael is familiar with it?"

"I hope you brought your own food, unless you're a fan of twenty-year-old vegetable curry," Michael said.

His dad chuckled. "I think the Rescue Service has that part covered."

"Well, it all sounds like a lot of work," their mom said. "I bet you could use an extra pair of hands."

"Don't look at me," Peter said. "I have soccer practice three times a week all summer long."

"And I'm grounded until school starts," Michael said glumly. No videos, no games, plus lots of extra work around the house. His shoulders were still sore from scrubbing the sides of the shed in their backyard.

"That's true," their mom said thoughtfully. "But we didn't say exactly *where* you were grounded, did we?"

"No," their dad said. "I don't think we did."

"So it seems to me that spending a few weeks at the station later this summer would still be appropriate."

Michael stared at his mother. Had she really said what he thought she'd said? "Wait—do you mean that? I can go visit him?"

"Don't get *too* excited," she said. "You'll still be grounded, which means it will be less like a vacation and more like an unpaid job."

Michael hugged her, looked up at her face to make sure she was really serious, and then hugged her again. "Thank you!"

"In the meantime, if you so much as *think* about sneaking out anywhere, the deal is off," she said, her voice catching in her throat. "Got it?"

"I'll keep an eye on him," Peter said. When he saw his mother's warning look, he quickly added, "Better than I did last time."

"I could use a little help with this bag," their dad said. "Michael, do you mind carrying it out for me?"

Michael grinned. "Sure."

His mom squeezed his shoulder, and then she turned to his dad and kissed him on the cheek. "Be careful. We'll see you when you get back."

"Bye, Dad," Peter said. As he walked back toward the train station with their mother, he glanced back over his shoulder at Michael and gave him a little wink.

"You should see the plans for the new station," Michael's dad said. "It's going to be huge. The Rescue Service is talking about building a new academy there, too. In a few years, when you're better, I bet they'll put you up there."

There were those words again: *when you're better.* Michael nodded but didn't answer.

His dad looked at him quizzically. "Did I say something

wrong? Don't you still want to join the Service?"

"No, I do," Michael said. "Or at least, I think I do."

"Then what's wrong?"

It took Michael a moment to find the right words. "I don't like talking about what will happen when I'm better."

"I don't understand," his dad said. "Why?"

"Because all it does is make me think about what will happen if I *don't* get better."

"You're making great progress," his dad said. "Of course you'll get better."

"I'm learning how to live with it," Michael said. "But I'm never going to be completely cured. And right now it feels like every time I have a panic attack, I'm letting you down."

Now it was his dad's turn to not answer. He pursed his lips and looked at Michael with an unreadable expression. "You think you're disappointing me because you have panic attacks?" he said finally.

"I wish I was more like you and Peter," Michael said. His voice was hoarse. "But I'm not, and I'm never going to be."

His dad started to say something and then stopped. He paused for a moment, then he knelt down and searched through his duffel bag. He pulled out his screen and handed it to Michael.

"What's this?" Michael asked.

"My report to the Rescue Service. Read the last two paragraphs."

Michael scrolled down to the end.

For risking his life to help preserve the lives of others during the flare, the Rescue Service will posthumously award Commander Randall Clarke its highest honor: the Silver Star of Valor.

He looked up at his dad. "He deserved it. Even though he'd probably tell you it was a waste of metal."

His dad nodded. "Keep reading."

Michael continued to the next section.

We would also like to recognize the actions of Michael Prasad and Lilith Colson, who, though not themselves members of the Rescue Service, repeatedly demonstrated its highest traditions of bravery, ingenuity, and selflessness.

"You don't ever need to be like me, or Peter, or anyone else," his dad said. "You don't need to stop having panic attacks or go into the Rescue Service. Just keep being yourself. Whatever you end up doing with your life, I'm going to be proud. And I promise you, people are going to take notice."

Michael nodded wordlessly. A ground-crew member came by to pick up the duffel bag, but Michael's dad shook his head. "We've got it."

Michael darted past him into the prep room and grabbed a suit. He put it on quickly and slung a small air tank over his shoulder. When he came out, his dad furrowed his brow and rubbed his eyes.

"Airlock dust," he mumbled, putting on his helmet. "Always gets to me. . . ."

Michael blinked and looked around. He hadn't noticed any dust in the air. They cycled the airlock and stepped out onto the surface. The air was calm and the sky was a beautiful pinkish yellow. Michael followed his dad out to the landing pad and set the duffel bag down next to the jumpship's gangway.

"Take care of yourself, okay?" his dad said.

He wrapped his arms around Michael and squeezed him tightly. Michael pressed his head against his dad's chest and hugged him back. They stayed that way for a long time, and then finally Michael let him go and jogged back toward the colony. His dad gave him one last wave, and then the gangway retracted and the cabin doors closed. Smoke billowed out from the engine, and a few moments later the ship lifted off.

Michael craned his neck back and watched it rise, balanced delicately on a bluish-white jet of fire. He followed the path of the ship, higher and higher, until it was nothing more than a pale dot of light like a solitary star in the sky.

"Bye, Dad," he said quietly. "See you soon."

AUTHOR'S NOTE

SOMETIME SOON, THE first astronauts will set foot on Mars. Within our lifetimes, men and women will be living there full-time, and by the end of this century, the first children will be growing up on another planet. As much as possible, I've tried to be accurate about what life on Mars might be like. Human technology is always full of surprises, and someday, all the dangers of Mars will be conquered. But for many, many years, life there will be extremely dangerous.

The Martian atmosphere, which is not only poisonous but colder than Antarctica and thinner than at the top of Mount Everest, will always be a threat for colonists. In this book I've imagined thin, flexible suits with air filters that could convert the carbon dioxide of the atmosphere into breathable oxygen. It will be a long time before anything like these suits would be practical enough for everyday use. In the meantime, a Martian colonist would need to wear something much bulkier and always carry around an oxygen tank. Someday, though, suit technology will reach the point where even children can wear them safely, and going out on the surface will be no more dangerous than riding in a car.

Another challenge, which believe it or not is actively being worked on by engineers today, is what to do with human waste while in an environment suit. If you think the suits worn by Michael and Lilith aren't especially practical in that department, then I won't argue. Instead, I'll refer you to NASA, who would appreciate any ideas you might have on the subject: In 2017 they sponsored a prize called the "Space Poop Challenge." I'm sure future generations of colonists will thank you!

Mars, which doesn't have a molten core at its center, doesn't have a magnetic field like Earth. This means compasses won't work, but much more important, it means solar radiation will be a significant danger. Earth's magnetic field helps redirect charged particles from the Sun away from the surface, and our thicker atmosphere absorbs a lot of the particles that slip through. A person living on the surface of Mars would be exposed to at least ten times the average dose of radiation that a person living on Earth receives. Worse, solar flares, which go almost unnoticed on Earth, could be very dangerous. Luckily, they won't be quite as bad as I've made them out to be in this book. Even the strongest flares aren't powerful enough to destroy satellites or cause immediate harm from radiation poisoning, and they usually only last for a few minutes. Still, the first colonies will probably be built underground to protect their inhabitants from radiation. Eventually, super-strong transparent domes might cover entire cities, and an artificially generated magnetic field might protect the entire planet from radiation.

Fortunately for future Earthlings, we now know that there are large deposits of frozen water on Mars. Some of the first evidence of underground ice was discovered in 2008 by the Phoenix lander that Michael and Lilith see in Chapter Four. Obviously, having a nearby source of water will be helpful whenever a colonist gets thirsty! But even more important, the "O" in "H_2O" stands for oxygen, meaning that water could be a major source of breathable air for environment suits and colonies. In fact, it's even possible that someday we might terraform Mars by liberating so much oxygen from the ice caps that the entire atmosphere becomes breathable.

Bits of modern technology that we take for granted will have to be rethought for Mars. Earth has an ionosphere, which is a layer of charged particles that reflects radio signals over the horizon, but on Mars, many communications will have to be relayed through satellites instead. Basically, if you can't see it, you can't talk to it! Because of the thin atmosphere, airplanes probably won't be practical on Mars, so I've imagined colonists traveling on rockets hopping around on ballistic arcs. If you like theme parks, you'll love flying like this: As soon as the rocket engines cut off, your flight will be like the downward plunge on the world's largest roller-coaster. *Passengers, please scream and prepare your tray tables for landing.*

Some of the greatest challenges, however, may be psychological. Early colonies will be small and claustrophobic, and people there will be cut off from the rest of humanity by a gap of fifty million miles. Panic disorder is a real condition that affects both adults and kids like Michael. But, like the millions of people on Earth today who suffer from panic attacks, humans on Mars will have the support of their friends, families, and medical professionals, and they will find ways to manage their fears and go about their daily lives. We are a resourceful and adaptable species, and in the end we always strive to expand what is possible, rather than letting ourselves be defined by our limitations.

Nobody knows yet who will be the first person to walk on Mars, or when that historic day will come. We don't know exactly what life on Mars will be like. But we can imagine, and we can dream, and we can look forward to the day in the not-too-distant-future when we will watch those first steps on our televisions and cell phones.

And who knows? Maybe *you* will be that first person. Maybe you will be the one who steps out onto the dusty surface of our sister planet, looks up at the pale blue dot of Earth, and sends back those first words.

We made it.

ACKNOWLEDGMENTS

WHEN YOU WORK on a book for almost seven years, you end up with a lot of people to thank.

I'm deeply grateful for the support of the writers who have mentored and encouraged me as I worked on this project. Michael and Lilith's story would be much more boring if it weren't for Shirin Bridges, who edited many drafts and commiserated with me over many more glasses of wine. Julie Artz, Sarahlyn Bruck, Amanda Conran, Phil Hickes, Connie Malko, Priscilla Mizell, Kendal Muse, Mikayla Rivera, Elizabeth Runnoe, and Wade Albert White all provided invaluable suggestions and encouragement. The awesome team of Heidi, Cameron, and Aidan Stallman gave me some of my best (and most enjoyable) beta-read feedback. And ever since a chance "anyone need a crit partner?" post, Cindy Dorminy has been an unwavering long-distance friend through a combined total of eight projects and counting. I hope I've done as much for these writers as they've done for me. Writing is a solitary business, and you need friends like these to keep you sane along the way.

A big thank-you to my agent, Bridget Smith at Dunham Literary, who has been a wonderful and enthusiastic partner. She's also the only person I know who has personally experienced the downward half of a jumpship ride, and how cool is that?

Many people shared helpful technical advice during the writing of this story. Anything that bears a resemblance to actual science is probably because of them; anything that I got wrong is my fault entirely. The smart folks at www.nasaspaceflight.com and www.cruisersforum.com corrected many important details, and Maria Michelle Vardanian of NYU Counseling Psychology provided extremely helpful feedback on anxiety and panic disorders. My friend Dr. John Malko was right about almost everything, though I offer what I believe is compelling evidence that print is not, in fact, dead.

When I was growing up, my family treated good books as treasures and joys to be shared. I'm especially grateful to my mother, Anne, who always pushed me to pursue a meaningful life while giving me room to discover what that meaning should be. As an adult I've learned a lot from my sister, Carrie, which makes me wonder how smart I would be if I'd started paying attention to her when we were kids. My extended family on both sides had an enormous impact on me, and while I don't have room to list them all, I'd like to especially thank Laurie and Stan Hawkins, who sparked my imagination time and time again when I was young.

I couldn't have begun a book like this without my children, Jack, Andrew, and Eleanor. The joy of being their father brought me back to writing after a long hiatus. Equally so, I couldn't have finished any book at all without the love and support of my wife, Kendra, who has made me happier than I used to think I had a right to be.

This book is dedicated to my father, Edward, who passed away before its completion. When I was a teenager, I overheard him saying that he thought I should pursue a creative writing degree instead of studying computer science, which astonished me so much that I actually did it. I hope he was as proud of himself, and of all the things he achieved, as he was of me.

READ ON FOR A SNEAK PEEK AT THE NEXT ADVENTURE FROM CHRISTOPHER SWIEDLER

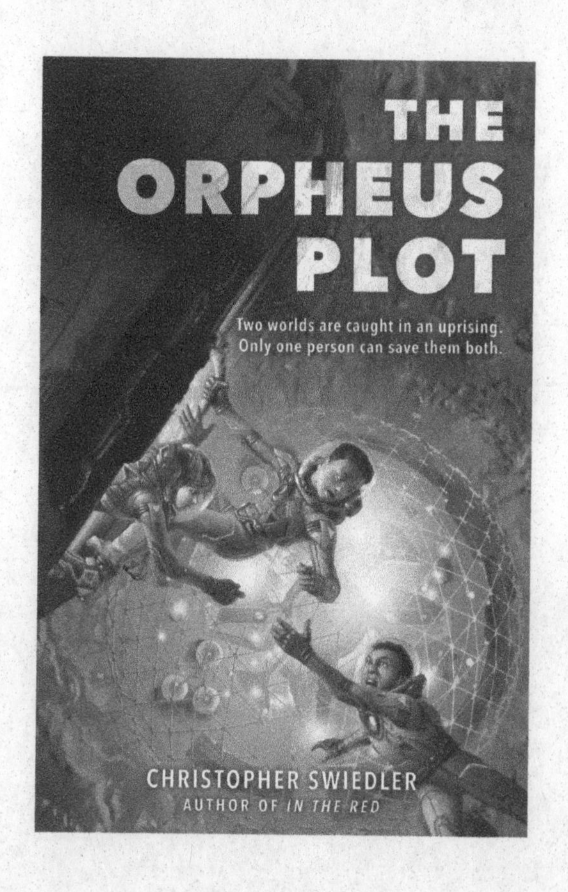

1

IF YOU GET caught, I'm going to pretend I don't know who you are.

Lucas stared at the message scrolling across his wrist screen, shielding it with his hand to keep the light from being noticed. He dictated a quick response to his suit's computer, keeping his voice low even though it was physically impossible for anyone else to hear him through the vacuum of space. *This was your idea, remember?*

Tali's response came quickly: *Then do me a favor and don't get caught.*

Lucas poked his head out from his hiding spot behind an empty fuel tank and looked around. The sun had set a little while ago and wouldn't rise again for another nine hours. In the starlight, the surface of the asteroid was a dark, dusty gray, pockmarked with shadowy microcraters. Off to one side, the skeleton of a ten-person rover that the colony kids used as a play structure glinted silvery white. A small row of blue lamps on the wall ahead of him marked the retractable doors of the naval hangar. It was after midnight, colony time, and if anyone saw him out here they were going to have a lot of questions that Lucas wouldn't want to answer. He needed his sister to stop sending him stupid messages and get down here to let him inside.

Why was she taking so long? *She'd* been the one to message *him*. He couldn't even remember the last time that had happened. Her schedule as a cadet on the teaching ship *Orpheus* meant they only got to see each other every few months. And even when she was here on Ceres at the same time as him, she was usually too busy studying or prepping for the upcoming term to spend much time with him. But then earlier today, out of the blue: *I have a surprise for you. Meet me at the hangar at 0130.* And then, a few seconds later: *You're going to like it.*

Lucas grinned. He could guess exactly what her "surprise" would be.

He felt the low rumble of airlock pumps cycling, and after an agonizingly long wait, the hangar doors slid open wide enough for him to slip inside. He squinted in the sudden brightness of the overhead lights. Military transports, scouts, and cargo haulers were lined din neat rows, all polished to the traditional Navy shine. He ran his hands along the hull of a sleek courier ship. It wasn't much more than a single-seat cockpit strapped to a pair of big engines. What would it be like to fly something like *this*?

He found his adopted sister, Tali, leaning against a desk at the back of the hangar. She was wearing the red-and-white uniform of a naval cadet—the same uniform he'd imagined for himself so many times. A thick bundle of cables ran from a computer screen on the desk to the cockpit of an old patrol ship, where a hand-lettered sign read SIMULATOR TIME LIMITED TO THIRTY MINUTES WHILE OTHERS ARE WAITING.

"Finally," she said, yawning.

"Finally, yourself," he shot back. "I was waiting out there twenty minutes."

She shrugged. "My roommate wouldn't fall asleep."

"So—any suggestions for a packing list?" he asked, abandoning the pretense that he didn't know what her surprise was. He knew he should probably ask her how she was doing or engage in some other kind of small talk, but right now he didn't have the patience.

Two days ago, his news feed monitoring program had alerted him that an outbreak of measles—*measles!*—had forced a transport ship from Earth to turn back. A cross-reference of the passenger manifest had confirmed that a thirteen-year-old girl on board was scheduled to be enrolled on the *Orpheus*. Naval immunization rules meant that she would have to miss the upcoming term, which meant that there was suddenly an open spot with nobody to fill it.

He'd sent in his own application on his thirteenth birthday, and he had nothing to show for it but radio silence. But now, with the recommendation of a senior cadet like Tali . . .

"Packing list?" she asked, frowning.

"I'll get my own uniform, right? But I can't find anything online about whether the Navy provides underwear. You'd think they'd be more clear about details like that."

"Wait," Tali said slowly. "You think the surprise is that I've gotten you onto the *Orpheus*?"

It was well done, he thought. She might have a second career as an actor if the Navy didn't work out. "Stop kidding around. It's not funny."

"Lucas, I'm not kidding. The surprise is that I got you time on the simulator. I thought it would be a fun thing to do before I shipped out."

He suddenly felt as if he'd been dropped into free fall. *This* was why she'd called him down here? So he could practice flying in a stupid video game?

"Lucas, I've told you this over and over," she said. "I can't get you into the academy. It's impossible."

"But there's an empty spot—"

"—which they're *not going to fill with a kid from the Belt.*"

"That doesn't make any sense!" Lucas said. "You're from the Belt!"

Tali shook her head. "I was born on Mars. That's totally different."

Totally different? She'd only been six years old when she'd moved here from Port Meridian on Mars. Not long after that, her parents had died, along with Lucas's mother, in the Tannhauser pressure dome accident here on Ceres. Afterward, Lucas's father had adopted her, and she'd lived with them for almost seven years. Most of her life had been spent in space. How was she any less of a Belter than he was?

"You need to stop getting your hopes up," she said. "The Navy has *never* accepted a Belter cadet. Do you think that's an oversight? Or just bad luck?"

Tali's voice had that same I-know-what-I'm-talking-about tone that she'd used to lecture him with when they were growing up on their father's mining ship. She liked to pretend that she was the expert on everything just because she was three years older than him. He'd forgotten how much he hated that tone in her voice.

"Did you even try?" he said, unable to keep the anger out of his voice. "Or were you just lying when you said you'd put in a recommendation for me?"

"I tried," she insisted. "Of course I tried. I talked to anyone who would listen. It was no use."

Was she telling the truth? Or was she just telling him that so he'd shut up and stop asking? Half of him suspected that was exactly what she'd done, while the other half hated himself for not trusting her.

"I know it sounds like it would be great to go to the academy," she said. "But it's hard enough for a kid from Earth or Mars. For you . . ."

Lucas knew that Tali was a lot better at social niceties than he was. Growing up on a mining ship meant spending a few days each month in port with whatever group of kids happened to be there at the time, and so you either got really good at making friends quickly, or you spent a lot of time alone. Lucas was solidly in the second category, and it had only gotten harder once Tali had left and he hadn't been able to rely on attaching himself to her and the friends she made. And sure, it would be even weirder being on a ship where he was the only Belter. But that wasn't going to stop him from joining!

"I'd be okay," he insisted.

"How would you know?" Tali asked. "Literally everything you know about Earthers comes from movies. Trust me—you really don't want to be at that school."

"You sound just like Dad," he muttered.

She stiffened. "Well, he's right. About this, anyway."

Tali and Tomas Adebayo were nothing alike, except for the million ways that they were *exactly* alike. Lucas noticed, and not for the first time, that Tali's reaction when he mentioned her adopted father was almost identical to the way their dad reacted when Lucas talked about *her.*

Suddenly he missed his sister, which was an odd feeling considering she was standing right in front of him. But what he missed wasn't Tali the cadet, but Tali the girl he'd grown up with. The one who had taught him how to use air ducts to sneak from one side of the colony to the other. The one who had taught him to fly *with style,* as she liked to put it. When she'd joined the Navy, it was as if those parts of her had just vanished. Now sometimes it seemed as if the only thing left inside her was anger. Anger at the Navy whenever she ran into some stupid regulation that she didn't agree with. Anger at Belters, especially miners, who she now seemed to think were some kind of primitive culture that she'd managed to escape from. But above all, anger at their father.

"How about we make a deal?" Lucas said suddenly. "I'll never, ever talk to you about joining the Navy again. I won't ask for any more favors or recommendations. I won't bug you about any of it. I just need you to do one thing."

Tali looked at him skeptically. "What's that?"

"Go see him."

He knew exactly how she'd react to *that* suggestion. Which, he supposed, was why he made it.

"You'd do that? Never ask about the Navy again? And all I'd have to do in exchange is go talk to Tomas?"

Lucas nodded. He didn't even have to consider it for a second. The rift between his father and his sister hurt him a hundred times more than not getting into the academy. And the extra, bonus, cherry-on-top stupidity of it all was that he knew it hurt Tali and his dad just as much. They were just too boneheadedly stubborn to admit it.

"Sorry, Lucas. It's not going to happen." She turned and opened up the simulator's canopy. "So are you going to get some practice time in, or what?"

Maybe she and his father were right. Maybe this was all stupid, trying to get accepted as a Navy cadet. He probably ought to just study piloting here on Ceres, like his dad wanted him to do.

Except that wasn't what *he* wanted. Flying little mining trucks was fun, and he was good at it—even Tali had to admit that. But what he dreamed about was piloting the big starliners and cruisers like the *Orpheus*. No apprenticeship in the Belt was going to teach him that. His dad hated the Navy as much as any Belter, but even he agreed that the best capital-ship pilots, hands down, were trained in the Navy.

Lucas turned and looked at the little courier that had caught his attention earlier. It certainly wasn't a cruiser, but it was a lot better than the boats he was used to flying. Maybe there was a way to salvage at least *something* out of tonight.

"Can I sit in it?" he asked Tali, pointing at the courier. "Just for a minute?"

She sighed. "Lucas . . ."

"It can't hurt anything to just *sit,* can it?" he said. "You owe me that much."

Tali frowned, clearly weighing the risks against whatever obligations she still felt toward him. "All right," she said finally. "But if you get caught—"

"You'll pretend you don't know who I am," Lucas finished. "I know."

He ran back to the courier and opened the canopy. Carefully he climbed into the cockpit and settled into the seat. The ship was so new that half of the controls were still covered in plastic wrap. The gauges and controls were all familiar to him from the mining trucks he was used to flying, but at the same time, everything felt completely different. Nothing was scratched up, bolted on, or hanging loose. Everything was in its proper place instead of being jammed in wherever it could fit.

His heart soared just being in a ship like this. It was practically *begging* to be flown. He flipped the main power switches, and the console sprang to life. Diagnostic messages flashed and status lights turned green. He imagined what it would be like to take her out. *If only . . .*

His reverie was shattered by a squawk over his suit's comm system. "Who's turning on my ship?"

Lucas's heart leaped into his throat. *Who . . . what . . . ?* He turned and saw a tall, silvery-haired woman in a blue-and-gold pressure suit striding toward them. Her name tag read Moskowitz. He didn't know who she was, but she was clearly an officer, which meant that he had slightly less than ten seconds of freedom left. Tali looked back and forth between Lucas and the woman, clearly trying to come up with some explanation for what they were doing here.

"Good evening, ma'am," she managed.

The woman stopped and cocked her head at Lucas. She was still a few meters away, and from that distance, the canopy and helmet were probably obscuring his face. Not knowing what else to do, Lucas gave her his best impression of a Navy salute.

"Did you sign up for the night shift?" Moskowitz asked Tali. "I don't remember seeing you on the list."

"Not exactly, ma'am," Tali stammered. "But I thought you might need help."

Moskowitz turned toward Lucas. "You're the new test

pilot? I know I said it was high priority, but I didn't expect you to show up in the middle of the night."

Test pilot? Something perked up in the back of Lucas's mind. Maybe there was a way out of this after all.

"Uh, yes, ma'am," he said, deepening his voice by an octave. What did test pilots sound like, exactly? "Like you said—high priority."

"But we can come back tomorrow," Tali said, giving Lucas an angry glance that he had no difficulty interpreting. "I'm sure now is not a good time for—"

"Oh, I'm not complaining," Moskowitz said. She tapped for a moment at the tablet she was carrying. "This way I won't have to wait until the day shift to get my test results. Push her hard, and do your best to max out the gee forces. I think the hiccup in the starboard engine is fixed, but we won't know until she gets out there."

Lucas grinned. This was even better than he'd hoped. She was actually asking him to *fly* this ship! As if in answer, Moskowitz waved her hand at the hangar doors. "Come on, now. I'm still planning on getting some sleep tonight. Take her out and tell me how that engine does."

Tali turned toward Lucas, her eyes wide, and gave him a tiny but emphatic shake of her head. "Get out now," she mouthed.

He grinned and put his hands on the controls. He

couldn't disobey a direct order from an officer, could he? And anyway, if he opened the canopy, Moskowitz would see that he wasn't even a cadet, much less an actual test pilot.

Ignoring Tali's furious glare, he angled the engines so that they were pointing down and inched the throttle forward. Under his control, the ship lifted off gracefully and hovered a few meters above the hangar floor. He pushed the control stick forward, and the ship soared out through the hangar doors and up toward the stars.

This was flying! Her thrust was only at a few percent of her max and she was already breaking free of the asteroid's gravity. He banked left and flew in a circle above the colony. The main dome glowed a brilliant yellow, with the half-circle of the naval base barely visible around it.

Lucas tilted the ship back until his engines were pointed straight down and jammed the throttle to its limit. Gee forces squeezed him against the seat as the ship leaped up into the night sky. The bright yellow disk of the sun appeared off to his left, and his helmet darkened to compensate for the additional light. He flipped her around quickly and used full thrust to brake to a halt.

"No need to showboat," Moskowitz said over the radio. "How does she feel? Any stutter on that starboard side?"

"She feels fantastic," he answered truthfully. "Smooth as silk."

"All right, then. Put her through a few turns and see how she handles."

He made an experimental S-turn and then rolled the ship onto her back. She responded to every movement of the control stick without a hint of balkiness or lag. He tested rolls, banks, dives, and climbs, momentarily forgetting everything except the joy of flying a ship like this.

As he rose higher and higher above the surface, he caught sight of a gleaming white shape high above: the teaching ship ISS *Orpheus,* where Navy cadets spent their first three years. The cruiser looked both elegant and deadly, with clean lines and polished transplastic windows that made his father's ship, the *Josey Wales,* seem like the back end of a garbage transport.

In less than twenty-four hours, the *Orpheus,* along with Tali and the rest of her students, would be heading out for the next term's cruise. Lucas felt a surge of anger. How many of those first-year cadets from Earth or Mars or Luna knew anything at all about being in space? Half of them were probably sick from free fall and the other half would still be trying to figure out how to brush their teeth in zero gee. It wasn't even the tiniest bit fair.

"All right, that's enough," the officer said. "Come on back in and I'll run some diagnostics."

"Yes, ma'am," Lucas answered, trying to keep the disappointment out of his voice. He flew one more ring around the *Orpheus* and then headed back to the naval base. As soon as he landed, Moskowitz closed the doors and repressurized the hangar.

"Nice flying," she said. "A little flashy, but I got the data I wanted."

Lucas paused. How was he going to get out of the ship without her seeing him? Tali, recognizing his predicament, tightened her jaw and looked around. They needed some kind of distraction. . . .